Puffin Books

Editor: Kaye Webb

Hengest's Tale

Long, long ago the Jutish king's daughter, Hildeburg, questioned young Hengest about Finn, the Frisian prince to whom she was promised in marriage. What sort of man was he – did he want her only for her dowry, she asked. Then Hengest replied, 'Finn is brave and honest, generous to all, and in all ways such a man as I would like to serve; you need not fear him. His hair is like flame, his eyes are like the morning mist, he is tall and he is young. Indeed I wish that I were such a man as he is.'

Happy marriage indeed, they all thought, that cemented the friendship between the Frisians and the Jutes with such a well-matched pair. But bitter sorrow, savage grief, lay in the future, when Hoc the Jutish king died and his son Hnaef the Half-Dane returned to claim his birthright, with his crude Danish followers who insulted and despised his father's thanes, so that many of them fled to Finn's court for protection. Cruel the rancour, bitter the woe, when Hnaef himself came to visit Finn's court, and Hildeburg had cause to mourn the deaths of a son and a brother in the fighting that broke out. Heavy and cold the truce, heavy and cold the winter, and bitter the memory still when Hengest the old man lay dying.

Jill Paton Walsh, author of *The Dolphin Crossing*, has here pieced together the haunting, puzzling scraps of an ancient legend. A strange, violent tale suitable for older readers – eleven upwards.

Cover design by Philip Gough

Hengest's Tale

Jill Paton Walsh

Illustrated by Janet Margrie

Penguin Books

Penguin Books Ltd, Harmondsworth,
Middlesex, England
Penguin Books Australia Ltd, Ringwood,
Victoria, Australia

First published by Macmillan 1966
Published in Puffin Books 1971

Made and printed in Great Britain by
Richard Clay (The Chaucer Press) Ltd,
Bungay, Suffolk
Set in Linotype Plantin

To Elaine

Prologue

This is a new story made out of the broken pieces of an old one. The broken pieces of the story are in the very oldest English poetry, written long before the Norman Conquest. It is not easy to see how they should fit together, and many scholars have worked hard to make sense of them without being able to agree with one another. It is not even known for certain, though it is possible, that the Hengest in the old story is the same as the real Hengest who conquered Kent, and is to be found in the history books.

I am not a scholar, but I like this story, and so I have put it together as best I can, and filled the gaps with new bits of my own, and written it down for you to read.

Nobody knows how it should really be told; but it might perhaps be like this.

Chapter One

Wanderer though I am, I have made my last journey now. I shall not again get even as far as the door of my own hall until they carry me through it. So I lie here remembering many things which sprang from the first journey I ever made. The memory is grim and bitter, more painful than my wounds, which trouble me little now. My women have staunched the bleeding, and poured balm into the gashes, but there is no balm for a heart which rages at the past. My curse on that first journey! My curse on its success! If my enemies in this land understood me they would curse it too. Instead they curse me for an oath-breaker, and a murderer. But though I am both these things, it is not blood shed, nor oaths broken in this land which break my rest. My heart was dead before ever I came here, and I care little enough for anything good or ill I have done since then.

I will tell you what I have done, so that you may make a fine song out of it, and keep my name alive after my death. It began with a journey long ago. There were twelve of us in the party. We were dangerously few for such an enterprise, but we dared not take a larger number, in case that seemed hostile to those we sought. I was just out of my boyhood, and I went with Wihtgils, my father, who led us, the others being four of King Hoc's thanes, and a servant for each of us. We were well armed, and mounted on the best horses Hoc's stables could provide, and we took no pack animals because although we carried things of importance we had nothing heavy or bulky, and we needed to travel fast.

The first part of our journey lay through our own lands, and we travelled without fear, staying in the halls of our friends. This part of the country had not been ravaged in the disasters of the past winter, and the spring was breaking out upon it. I remember it seemed a good land to live in, and it was hard to remember the threat which hung over it. Besides, it was all new to me, and I was at an age when one does not think dark thoughts for long, and all new things bring joy to one's heart. Through all the discomforts and uncertainties of that journey, I found it easy to be cheerful.

As we approached the end of Hoc's domain the country became less inhabited. The level of the land dropped, and the ground became marshy underfoot. There were no thanes' halls to sleep in at night, but we had to make do with the poor huts of peasants, full of the warmth and stench of their cattle. We turned south from the westerly route we had been following, till we reached higher ground, and thick forest. Then we turned west again, following an ancient path kept open by the elves perhaps, for it was easy to follow though we saw no travellers on it but ourselves.

Three days' journey through the forest brought us to a river. Beyond it, my father said, lay the land of the Frisians to whose king we were going. But we were a long way from our destination yet, for the king of the Frisians kept his court on the far side of his wide kingdom, and we had little enough reason to suppose his people would treat us as friends. And it took us another two days to find a ford. It was a bad ford too – the current was swift, so we had to dismount and wade across waist deep in water that was icy from the snows melting on some distant hills. The old men in our party were so afflicted by the crossing that we had to stop and light a fire at once so that they could sit huddled over it shivering their limbs into warmth again. My father was young for his years, but he too was not sorry to draw close to the fire with them, while I stood scornful of such necessities, gazing back at the homeland we had left, with my damp kirtle stuck to my ribs and my skin smarting in the cold wind.

It was another day before we came to the first Frisian settlement. It lay in a clearing in the forest, and was much like the homesteads of our own churls – a long thatched house, a cattle pen, a small field of barley, and an acre of pasture. At the house door a woman and a child stood staring at us. My father hailed the man of the house, who sat mending a broken halter. The man's answer was gruff, and in a strange tongue. But my father seemed to understand him, and explained to him that we were strangers, and in need of provisions, for which we would pay in silver coin, and of directions so that we might find our way through the forest. Listening to the conversation I found that I could just understand it; the Frisian tongue was a near cousin to mine. The churl was suspicious, but cautious too; careful lest we were enemies, but not wishing to give offence to harmless strangers. He asked questions, but from my father he got vague answers only. We were travellers from the east, seeking the court of King Folcwald for reasons of our own. He admitted less, indeed, than our clothes and manner of speaking must have revealed; by these we were marked as Jutes for all to see.

We got the food and fresh water we needed, and shelter for the night inside his wooden fence, so that we could sleep without leaving a guard against wolves. And the next day he sent one of his slaves to show us to the edge of the forest.

Once we were out of the forest we found ourselves on rolling open heathland, with few people living on it, and those mainly farmers and fowlers. The way to Dorestead was not hard to find, and we rode along it by day, and camped beside it at night. I well remember how careful we were. The first man in the party rode a little ahead, carrying a white pennant at the tip of his spear. We answered all questions as we had answered the churl of the forest. Our food we bought from the villagers, paying without question whatever they asked, even when it was exorbitant. Most of them asked for a fair price. The wisdom of coming in a small party was now apparent, for none could suppose we meant harm, being so few. At night we camped and lit our fires by the road like men who have nothing to fear, making no attempt at concealment. We set a man on guard of course, though we were too few to ward off attack.

I think we had been in Frisia about three days when we first saw the riders. There were about thirty of them, riding on the brow of a hill above the road, in the same direction as ourselves, and as soon as we sighted them, they disappeared behind the crest. Once we glimpsed them on our right, riding in good order through a little wood, and disappearing in the trees within moments of being seen, and once we came to the ford of a little stream, and saw them a good way downstream on our left, watering their horses. We did not like the look of them for they were well armed, and outnumbered us by nearly three to one. Besides, we could not guess what they were doing, unless they were following us, and they made us uneasy. Perhaps they were waiting for us to fall into a trap. Yet had they wished they could have overpowered us at once.

As the days passed, and we caught constant glimpses to remind us of their presence, and they made no move against us, the strain told on our nerves, and we became fretful and bickered among ourselves. Only my father remained calm, yet he must have found it hardest to bear, for he knew best how much depended on our success; how much in lives, and in honour for our king; and it was my father who had promised the success of this embassy, pledging himself so deeply that not all his long years of service would save him from disgrace if we should fail.

King Folcwald, whom we sought, kept court at Dorestead, in the far south of his kingdom, a journey of ten days from the frontier. For the first five days we rode and slept unmolested, though the riders followed us all the way.

On the fifth night disaster struck. We were awakened by the sound of hooves at a gallop, and awoke to see our horses being ridden away in the moonlight, their halters tied together so that three men could take them all. As we sprung to our feet shouting, and groping for weapons, the moon slid behind a cloud, and the whole scene was plunged into darkness. We ran about, shouting angrily, each of us searching for his pack, and as our fire had died down to a few hot ashes and we could see nothing, it was some minutes before we found the poor fellow we had left on guard, lying beside the embers with his throat cut open.

Our concern for our murdered companion occupied us for some time, but we soon became aware of our plight. We were alone on a deserted path in enemy country, without horses, and stripped of our weapons, and all our possessions. We had not even a water bag left. For the rest of the night we sat huddled together, not daring to light a fire, not daring to go to sleep. Once or twice the moon slipped through the scudding cloud, and by her pallid light we found one spear which the thieves had left – one spear between eleven men.

At last dawn broke, and we dug a grave for our dead man and then trudged on, hungry and thirsty and on foot, and angry at the indignity of our loss. Were we to arrive like beggars at Folcwald's court? Were we to sell our cloaks and daggers to buy food? As we went we uttered curses on the brutal men who followed us day and night, and then sneaked their advantage in darkness, instead of giving us the chance to fight, desperate though that chance would have been. Our very lives now depended upon finding friendship among the Frisian peasants, and now that things had gone wrong we all remembered that the Frisians had been enemies rather than friends to our people.

It must have been early in the afternoon that the trees of the wood we were crossing began to thin out, and the air to lighten. Ahead of us somewhere there was a clamour of birds, wheeling and cawing in the still air. I remember looking up, and seeing the dark shape of a raven floating above the branches with wings outspread.

Then suddenly the path ran out of the wood into the open, and the unbroken sunlight glared golden beyond the speckled shade of the last trees. And against the sun, thrown into sharp relief were three dark shapes – the terrible shapes of three men hanging from the lowest branch of the last tree. The birds had already settled on the shoulders of one of them, and at our approach a jackal slunk away into the brush.

We stopped short, terrified. At last my father said,

'They at least will not hurt us,' and started forward. As

we reluctantly drew near we saw under the gently swinging feet of each man a pile of something which glittered in the sun. There on the ground below them lay our shields and packs, our swords and spears, and the royal casket, with Hoc's seal unbroken on the lock. Just beyond the gallows tree our horses were grazing peacefully, tethered to a thorn bush. Dumb with astonishment we collected our burdens together, and passed the water bottles round, relief flooding over us. As I tilted my head to drink I looked up, and saw the riders, on a little rise in the ground ahead of us, sitting motionless in their saddles, and looking towards us. Their leader rode a black horse, and wore a cloak of magnificent purple, and his head seemed to glitter in the sun. I raised my arm and pointed to them, and they turned their horses' heads and rode away at once.

'Who can they be, Father,' I asked, 'who find and punish thieves, and keep none of the spoil for themselves?' For there had been nothing missing from our things. My father could not answer my question; but whoever the strangers were we feared them no more.

We soon had other things to worry us, for the next day the character of the country changed, and we found ourselves in low, flat, marshy country, with greener and richer pasture than any I have ever seen, but dangerous for strangers, because of the quagmires and oozy swamps which spread across it. In places the path was built upon a causeway, but in others it wandered through rushy meadows, or ran across marshy places where we were afraid of losing it and sinking to our deaths. Yet there were many more villages here than there had been in the heathlands, and everywhere sleek cattle were grazing. The villages were built on raised mounds to keep them above the level of floods, and more astonishing to me than the richness of the country was the fact that the settlements were unfortified so that for many miles together the only earthworks we saw were dykes. So great was Folcwald's power that his people dwelt secure in open country. And they were more friendly than the folk of the lonely heath, so that we slept under roofs as guests for the next few nights. Our hosts were only farmers, but we were

comfortable enough with them, for they had large tall houses, and they ate and drank well. More striking still was the fine cloth of which their clothes were made, and the splendid bowls and dishes in which their food was served. They had in plenty red pottery of fine smooth make and lovely shapes, stuff which in our country would have graced the tables of the king.

Compared with the poverty in which our farmers lived these people seemed like a race of thanes to me; and their wealth had given them some of the tastes of thanes too, for they entertained us with good songs, and had proud manners, as though they were men of note. My father said that most of Frisia was country of this kind.

In this rich and happy country disaster struck us for the second time. We were riding through a wide expanse of swamp, following the path as best we could. For some time we had seen nothing of the riders, though the paths were so many, and so heavily fringed with rushes, that they might have ridden unseen only a hundred yards away. Wulfhelm, my servant, was riding ahead, carrying the white pennant. Suddenly there was a snake on the path, hissing fiercely at the disturbance. Wulfhelm's horse reared, and bolted off the path. Horse and rider together at once started to sink into the quagmire beside the path, while we stood helpless and horrified onlookers. The terrified animal struggled desperately, sinking all the faster, and screaming as it sank. Wulfhelm too was yelling, trying wildly to get clear of the horse before its struggles dragged him down too.

I slipped from my horse, and threw my shield out on to the mud. Then, shouting for someone to bring a rope, I jumped on to the shield. It held my weight, but I could not reach Wulfhelm. He was floundering about with only head and shoulders above the mud. He was silent now, and only the look in his eyes betrayed his fear. The screaming neigh of the horse stopped with sickening suddenness. I leant towards Wulfhelm, holding the end of the rope that had been thrown to me, but the shield tilted, and the mud started to ooze over the edge. Voices from the bank called to me to come back while I could. But I gingerly lowered myself, and knelt on the shield. Then I undid my cloak pin, and spread my cloak out on the mud before me. I was afraid, I think for the first time in my life, for I remember that I was surprised to find that fear is a cool hard feeling, which leaves the mind clear, and the limbs ready for action. I uttered a prayer to the gods, and stretched myself out, lying flat on my cloak. I felt it sink, felt the mud beneath it swell up round me, holding my body in a cold soft clasp. But it moved only slowly, and now I could reach Wulfhelm. I tied the rope to his wrists, for he was up to his neck now, and only his head and hands were above the surface. Then I left the party on the bank to haul him out, and thought only of myself. I pushed on my sinking cloak, and strained to raise myself upon my knees again. As I did so the shield at last began to sink, and the nauseating slime held me by the knees. I lay flat upon the surface again at once, and wriggled like a worm upon it, making painfully slow progress towards the bank. Luckily I was soon within reach of my father's spear held out to me, and he dragged me till I could crawl on to the firm pathway again. Wulfhelm was bcing dragged out by two of the horses pulling on the end of the rope, for it proved beyond the strength of our men to move him. He groaned with pain at the strain on his arms.

I sat on the bank, soaked to the skin, and reeking with the foul-smelling mud, and watched while he was slowly drawn to safety. Then something made me look up, and

I saw, beyond the pool of mire which had nearly killed us, on some firm ground at the other side, a mounted man, sitting in his saddle watching us. His horse was dark as night, and he himself wore a cloak of deep purple. His head was bright even in that misty place, for his hair was the colour of copper new from the smelting, and was bound with a circlet of gold. When he saw me look up he rode away through the rushes.

Wulfhelm was in a bad state when he was got out at last, shuddering and exhausted, and unable to move his arms. So we turned back to the village we had left a few hours before. I rode in the rear, conscious of the foul smell of my soaking clothes. My father dropped back and rode beside me. He did not speak, but I felt his approval and was glad.

We got dry clothes, and a place beside a good fire for Wulfhelm at the village, though they clearly thought us great fools for not keeping to the path. It took Wulfhelm three days to recover the use of his arms, and even then he could manage the reins of his horse only with difficulty.

For three days therefore we hung about, with nothing to do, and only gloomy thoughts to think. We were now only two days' journey from Dorestead, but we had met with poor luck so far. And doing nothing was bad for me, for it left me free to think about Hnaef, my cousin and my lord, who was now a captive in the land of the Danes.

I sat around thinking of the disaster that had overtaken us. I remembered how the miserable survivors of the terrible battle against the Danes had come back to be mocked and taunted and reviled by those whose brothers and sons and fathers had fallen. I remembered how the list of the dead seemed to carry the names of all the good and strong men of the land – the flower of the Jutes, the best of all Hoc's thanes. And I remembered the messengers of the Danes, with scornful words offering harsh terms for a truce; taking a sum of gold so great that we had to beg for seven years to pay it, and demanding as a hostage Hoc's only son, our prince, and my kinsman and friend. So Hnaef had gone into hostile lands, to the court of Sigehere, to the stronghold of the Danes. But before he was taken all the Jutes of Hoc's court had sworn to serve him after Hoc's death; and I, his kinsman, sharing with him the blood of the god, and born in the same year, had been the first to swear.

And now I kept brooding, remembering his pale face, and the tears of his sister Hildeburg, though whether she wept for her brother, for herself, or for me, I did not know. When I was not thinking about this I wondered who the stranger on the black horse could be; for my father had forbidden us to ask about him, saying that he plainly wanted to keep his name to himself, and intrusive curiosity ill became strangers.

At last we set off again, slowly, for we were short of a horse, and I had lent Wulfhelm mine, so the whole party were kept to the pace at which I could walk. Soon we came to the spot where the accident had happened – a place like almost any other stretch of path, but I recognized it at once. I knew even the angle at which a broken rush tilted at the mire's edge. But while I was looking at broken rushes the others were looking ahead. A little way farther down the path someone had driven a stake into the ground, and slung a shield on it. There was nobody in sight near it. And it was no ordinary shield – it had a boss and rim of gold, and was heavily wrought with dragons' and boars' heads. As we stood round looking at this princely thing we saw that it was not new but had a few dents in the wood, and the leather handle strap was worn.

'It is a gift for Hengest!' the men were saying. I looked at it doubtfully.

'What do you think of it?' I asked my father.

'I do not know,' he said. 'Take it if you will, for both the need of it and the risk are yours.'

'Then have it I shall,' I said, and swung it over my arm. I felt better at once, for it is a naked feeling to walk in a strange land without a shield. And I was pleased to carry a thing of such beauty. Nevertheless we did not feel the value of it till we came to the next village.

There the people stared at me keenly, and murmured among themselves. Then they went running to bring us bowls of fresh milk and loaves of new bread, presenting me with the largest share. They would accept no payment for the food they gave, and we had no difficulty in buying a horse from them, though we had met with flat refusal in the village we had just left. And although our need placed them at an advantage they asked only a fair price for the horse, and lowered it when they realized it was for me that it was wanted.

'Should the owner claim this shield,' I said laughing when we were beyond the last house of the village on our way again, 'it will certainly be worth a fight to keep it!'

'Wait till you see whom it is you must fight for it,' said my father smiling.

In the evening of the next day we came to Dorestead. It was in the soft light just before sunset. From far off we could see a patch of glimmering light, and beyond it the wide pale shimmer of a great river. As we drew nearer we could see that the city was built on a wide flat-topped hill rising just a little above the level of the river bank. And the glitter was scattered from a group of roofs at the top of the town, which seemed to be made of the purest gold. The evening mist from the river wound round the

walls of the town, so that it looked as if it floated on the silver water and I thought it must be the country of the elves we were come to. But the elves can ward off danger with the glance of their eyes; and the inhabitants of Dorestead had built walls to defend themselves. The walls too were wonderful, for they were built of stone, a thing I had never seen before. I think even my father was impressed by Dorestead. The sun was sinking as we gazed, and we hurried on, hoping to reach the gates before nightfall. As we rode my father pointed across the great river.

'There,' he said, 'is the land of the Romans. The Franks hold it now, but when I was a boy this was the frontier of the Roman king, who was the strongest and mightiest in the world.'

'Stronger than Folcwald?' I asked.

'Stronger many times than any king of the Frisians has ever been.'

'Stronger than Sigehere?'

'Able to crush the king of the Danes in a single summer, and use only a few of his soldiers to do it.'

'Then why did he let the Franks take his land? What became of him?'

'I do not know,' said my father. 'But he dwells in the far south. Perhaps he has turned his face from the north, and cares no more about these lands. There is a rich island called Britain, away in the western seas, which also belonged to him, and I hear he is gone from there too.'

That was the first time I heard of the land in which now I lie dying.

Chapter Two

By the time we reached the gates of the town it was dark, and we could see the walls only dimly looming above us. But the gates were still open, though guards were set at either side. We were not alone on the road; there were fisherfolk coming up the path from the river, carrying creels of fish, and talking cheerfully. They entered the gates without attracting the attention of the guards, but when we made to enter we were stopped and courteously asked our names, and our business.

'We are strangers from the east,' said my father, 'seeking to speak with King Folcwald.'

'No man is a stranger to himself,' said the sentry warily, 'yet a man has a right to keep his name unspoken if he wishes. But if you will not tell me who you are you must wait at the gate while we send to ask the king if he will receive nameless strangers.'

But at that moment I stepped forward and stood at my father's side. The sentry saw my shield, and his expression changed at once. He called to the captain, who came over, and seeing the shield bowed to us, and said,

'Come with me strangers, and I will take you to the hall of our king.' Then he led the way up the street, turning to my father as he went, to say, 'I have been a sentry at these gates for many years, but never before have I seen a party of strangers with a more goodly appearance both of the wisdom of age and the courage of youth! It will be a good thing for the Frisians that you have come.'

My father bowed in acknowledgement of these courtesies and we walked on. The streets were full of people returning from work in fields and on the river, and women stood talking at the doors, which were lighted with torches so that the streets were bright and gay. We caused a stir as we passed walking close together, fully armed in the footsteps of the captain of the gate. I heard people tell each other, 'These are the strangers!' 'Here are the Jutes!' and 'Finn says one of these men carries his shield.' 'Finn says the bravest of the Jutes bears his shield, look there he is!'

So it was, on the lips of his own people that I first heard Finn's name.

The sound of it followed us through the town right to the door of Folcwald's hall. But keenly though I was straining my ears to hear what was said of me and my shield, I was not prevented from seeing with amazement how many of the houses we passed had richly carved doorposts, and eaves adorned with painted dragons, which seemed to move in the flickering lights and shadows cast upwards by the torches.

And so we came to Gold-gleamer, Folcwald's great hall. By now it was too dark to see the outside of the hall, though we could make out its great size. The eaves overhung the door, making a covered threshold, and here the captain bade us wait. He was only a few moments inside before returning to lead us in. 'The king will receive you,' he said, 'but you must leave your weapons here.' Reluctantly we stacked our swords and spears against the wall, but we were not asked to lay aside shield or helmet.

So it was in the garb of a warrior, young and eager, and proud of my own name, that I entered Gold-gleamer for the first time. I had no foreboding of the bitterness and welling grief with which I would enter it again. Hatred and vengeance did not yet hold my heart in their grim grip.

And who could think of woe in such a place? The hall was large and fair. The walls were hung with tapestries of splendid weave, patterned with tales of the gods, and the roof beams were painted in many colours. Even the floor was of smooth-cut slabs of stone beneath the rushes; many the skilful hands which had made that hall! Sitting at their benches were Folcwald's thanes, feasting in comfort and comradeship and above them all, on a chair on a dais hung with purple sat Folcwald, and beside him on either hand sat a young man and an old man. The old man was wrinkled and bent with age, and the young man had hair the colour of copper, so that we knew him at once for the leader of the riders who had escorted us for so long.

Places were cleared for us at the line of benches, and we sat down facing the high-seat of the king.

'Greetings, strangers,' said Folcwald, 'you are welcome to my hall. Eat and drink, and listen to the song of the minstrel, and when you are rested and content you shall say who you are, and on what errand you have come.'

Food was set before us in fine dishes, and as we sat eating I looked around me eagerly, wondering at many things I had never seen before. The Frisians had their wives with them at the meal; whereas among our folk only the queen or princess ever entered the hall. But the Frisian women sat along the walls, each behind her husband or father, talking gaily to each other, waited on by slave boys, keeping a watchful eye on the men, and rising to take and fill the drinking-horn whenever it was drained dry. The tables were laden with red dishes of even finer make than those we had seen in the houses of farmers, the drinking-horns were encrusted with jewels and bands of gold, and there were cups of silver and of glass to be seen as well. The thanes wore clothes of many colours, red and saffron, and bright blue, which I had never seen before, making our clothes, dyed only with woodland berries, look poor and dull, though they would not have shamed us at home. The men's cloaks were not fastened at the neck like ours, but fastened on the shoulder, and falling in a great sweep to the knees. This way of wearing showed the fine cloth and costly dyeing to advantage, but I saw also that it left their sword arms free from all encumbrance. The women wore long white gowns, and fine brooches, and they had fillets of gold in their hair.

But though there were many things to look at in the hall my eyes kept going back to rest on Folcwald, and the young man who sat beside him. Folcwald was a sturdy man in the prime of his strength, with a grave face, a loud voice, and gusty laughter. The young man was graceful in manner, and had cool eyes of pale grey, in contrast to his blazing hair.

After a little while Folcwald's queen entered, and sat down near him. Then seeing that there were guests in the hall she rose and came among us with her maidens, bringing cups to set before us, and a pitcher to fill them. I hoped to taste good ale or mead again after having no strong drink on the journey, but the liquid poured from the queen's jars was neither golden nor brown, but red like a man's blood in water. It ran down my throat in a warm trickle, and glowed in my belly, and it tasted mellow and smooth.

'What is it?' I whispered to my father.

'It is wine,' he replied. 'The drink of the gods, which is brought down the great river from the far south. Do not drink deeply of it, for it is strong stuff, though it tastes gentle.'

All this time we were offered as much food as we could eat, and the minstrel sang bravely from the corner. Then the queen arose, and came to us again, this time bringing a basket full of precious things, which she shared among us as gifts. To my father she gave a little golden dagger, to me a drinking bowl of coloured glass, to all the others something fine and valuable. When we had all received something she turned to the thanes in the hall, and told them to compete with their lord in giving welcome to his guests.

And all the noblest of the thanes came forward, in turn each bringing some small gift; they gave cloak pins, jars of wine, coloured ribbons like those they wore round their brows, and all these things they laid before us. This must have been a custom among them, for they had gifts ready though we had arrived unbidden, and the speeches they made as they gave them had the ease of familiarity.

When the last gifts had been given, Folcwald addressed us again.

'Strangers, we hope that you are warm and rested in our hall, that you have eaten and drunk your fill, and that your hearts are gladdened by our gifts. And now if you are contented, stand and tell us who you are, and why you seek us.'

My father rose to his feet. 'I am Wihtgils, son of Witta, son of Woden the god. I am not unknown in the court of Hoc, king of the Jutes, nor is my name held in small honour there. My companions are trusted thanes of my king, and we seek you, Folcwald, with words of great weight to speak when you shall say the time to hear us is right. Great is the honour you have given

us as guests; may you not regret it when you hear us speak!'

'Son of Witta,' said Folcwald, 'it is not likely that I shall regret honour done to a man such as you, whose fame for wisdom and good counsel has spread far and wide. You are welcome here with all those you bring. Tomorrow I shall summon my advisers, and before them you shall unlock your word-hoard for all to hear.'

Then Finn stepped forward. To me he said, 'Stranger, where did you get that shield?'

'If it is yours,' I answered, 'take it back. But if you value it, do not leave it lying in lonely places, for should I find it again you will surely have to fight to get it back!'

He laughed. 'The strap is worn to fit my hand, and I have grown used to it,' he said, 'but give it to me with a willing heart, and I will exchange it for another one of greater worth. And tell me, O mud-walker, what is your name?'

'I am Hengest, son of Wihtgils,' I said.

'I am Finn, son of Folcwald,' he said, 'and Hengest mud-walker is welcome to these halls.' Then he brought a bench and sat beside me, and we drank together, and joked and boasted of our many skills, till the fires burned low, and the minstrel grew tired and ceased his song, and the thanes of Folcwald began to think of sleep. Beds were spread out for us in a warm part of the hall, and Folcwald went off to his own chamber, but Finn stayed with us, and made his bed near mine.

Perhaps I should have feared the future then, when a man I had meant to hate became my friend. But how can one hate brave and gracious ways? And then it made the task I had to face lie easier upon my heart.

The next morning I was woken by a groom stepping over my bed to shake Finn awake, and telling him that his horse was ready. I raised my head. The rest of our party were sound asleep, despite the pale light of dawn falling on their faces through the smoke holes in the roof. They were tired from the rigours of the journey, and the wine they had drunk last night.

'Will you ride with me?' whispered Finn, and I rose and went with him. Outside the door stood his black steed saddled and ready, and a fine grey stallion for me. We mounted, and rode through the town, making for the gate along with fishermen and farmers with whose homeward journey we had fallen in the night before. Those we passed greeted Finn cheerfully, and the sentry hailed me also as we passed. Once outside the town we rode down to the river bank, and then cantered westward through the mist.

'What say you,' asked Finn, 'shall we ride all day? Shall we go and look at the weather on the western sea?'

'Ride on!' I cried, 'and I will follow!'

So we rode all morning, sometimes at a gallop, sometimes slowly to rest our horses, while the sun rose over our heads, and the mist cleared, and we found ourselves in marshy country too wet for farming or even for pasture. But the path we rode on was well kept up, dry and firm. It ran within sight of the great river all the way, and there were lookout posts along it, all well manned. We came to a point where we could only just see the other bank of the river, it had grown so wide, and still we rode on.

Then half-way through the afternoon we came to the shore. There was a long spit of land, higher than the hinterland, running out to sea. On either side of it great breakers rolled on to golden beaches, tossing white spume which glittered in the sun. And along it was a row of three great mounds, which Finn said were the barrows built over the tombs of the kings of his house. We rode out to the third of them, which stood on the tip of the promontory, and there we left our horses to graze, while laughing and panting for breath we raced each other to the top. I won, for Finn missed his footing on the slippery fine grass, and rolled someway down again before he could stop himself. And there I stood, gazing in astonishment at the wide sea, streaked with white by the stormy wind, while Finn climbed up to me.

The wind, and our long ride without breakfast had made me famished, and I accused Finn loudly of starving his guests. But he brought out his pouch, and drew from it two round flat loaves, of good coarse filling bread, and we sat down to eat. When I bit into mine I found it had been spilt and spread with yellow honey, which ran down our chins and fingers as we chewed, so that when we had finished we clambered down to the beach to wash in the salt waves. Finn threw off his cloak and kirtle and plunged in, while I struggled to rid myself of the clumsy Jutish trousers which we wore laced to our legs. I was afraid of the wild water, but I scorned to show it, and so I waded in, and was knocked flying by the first tall wave I met, while Finn, who ducked and swam through them, laughed at me. I was glad to get out, for the turbulent water was cold as ice.

We dried ourselves as well as we could by rolling in the sandy grass, in which pink flowers grew in stout clumps, smelling fresh when we rolled on them. I left my leggings where they lay, and rode bare legged like Finn. And I pinned my cloak at the shoulder too, for I saw that instead of flying out behind him on the wind when he galloped, Finn's cloak was pressed against him warmly.

'What lies beyond this great sea?' I asked him, as we went in search of our horses.

'First there is Britain,' he told me, 'which was a Roman land for a long time, but is now left to its native folk. Beyond that there is another sea, and then a green island with rich pastures, and many kings fighting for it, and beyond that there is nothing but ocean for ten days' sailing at least. And further still there is only the end of the world.'

We found our horses grazing on the fine sea-grass, and on the sweet pink flowers, and we set off home at a brisk trot, for it was late, and we would miss our dinner even if we rode in the dark. But we had not gone far when Finn saw the fishing boats, a little fleet of them, making up river at good speed, running before a strong wind. He hailed them, waving his cloak over his head, and one of them put in to the beach, and picked us up. Finn paid one of the crew to take our horses home, and we sat in the bows of the boat, with

the water foaming under them, and splashing on our faces.

As we went Finn told me about the great river, which rose he said in the far south, in the land of the Roman king, and carried rich trade in Roman wares, like the pottery we had seen and fine cloth, which men brought to exchange for amber from Denmark, and furs and tin from Britain. The great wealth of his people was drawn from this trade, and from their skill as seamen. But now times were harder, because the wild Franks had settled between Frisia and Roman lands, and the disturbance they brought had made trade more risky and less profitable than it used to be.

And he told me of a great plan he had; he wanted to build a new town and stronghold in the far north of Frisia, where the land was almost empty of people because it was too swampy to farm. From this northern town the ships of Frisia could sail the sea-roads to Denmark and the far north, and trade down the coasts as far as a land called Spain. Then perhaps the Frisians could recover the trade they had lost when the Danes learned to send their amber south by an overland route.

'My father will not let me go and build my town, and invite merchants to live and work there, because he says it is too dangerous to live so far from his court, where protection would be hard to come by, and so near the frontiers with the Jutes who were once our enemies,' he said. I knew then that our embassy would succeed.

It did. We reached Gold-gleamer in the gloom of evening, and found that the meal was over, and Folcwald and my father each with his advisers were already in council in an inner chamber. With a rueful glance at the empty tables we went to join them.

All this was long ago; I cannot now remember the faces of all who sat there, nor the exact words which were spoken. I remember the gist of things well enough. Hoc had sent us to seek an alliance with the Frisians, and a promise of aid if the Danes attacked us again. The Frisians had no quarrel with the Danes, so we offered generous terms to help persuade them. Several of their wise men argued against us, saying it was foolishness to get oneself enemies where there were none before. Against this my father pitted all his cunning saying that a fight between Danes and Frisians was bound to come sooner or later, and it would be better when it did come that it should be defending our frontier, and therefore on our fields and farms, while the lands of Frisia lay safe behind the battle lines.

Great was my father's wisdom; yet this talk was all,

had we but known it, in vain; it was not in battle that the Jutes were to lose their freedom to the Danes. And for all my father's cunning words, it was the gifts Hoc offered which spoke for us best. To Folcwald he sent gifts of silver and of gold, of furs and of ivory, cunningly wrought. And to seal the treaty he offered the hand of Hildeburg, his daughter, to the son of the Frisian king, and for her dowry he offered the islands off the northern coast, which lay like a chain of beads running along their coast and ours, in the sea-roads of the north, in the very place where Finn wanted to build his new town.

I could see how tempting these offers were to the hearts of those who heard. They sat in silence, with hope and desire glinting in their eyes. But Folcwald hesitated.

'Among us a princess is betrothed young, and Hildeburg is already at an age to marry. Are your ways different? Or how is it she is not betrothed?'

'It is by my advice to my king,' said my father heavily. 'I have told him always to keep her free, to bind himself and his family to no alliance too soon, lest the times should change, and we should regret the friends we have chosen. But when I gave this advice' – he held his head high as he spoke – 'I always had it in my heart that one day I should remind my king of my long service, and ask for her for my son. For the blood of the gods runs in our veins, and we are not an unworthy line for him to join in bonds of kinship. But now our people are crushed by defeat, and many hopes and plans lie in the dust. I am not the only one who must go disappointed. I have changed the advice I gave. She is free of oath or bond. Finn may take her without making enemies.'

'A man may make an enemy by taking another man's hope,' said Finn, looking up at me.

Then I stood up and answered him. 'You shall not make an enemy of me, Finn. I will not hide what is in my heart. When I came here I came ready to bear a grudge. But I will bear no grudge against you, because I desire her good, and I see that you are the man to keep her from danger, and keep her heart in peace.'

Then Finn said, 'I will be glad to take a wife who is held in such honour by you, Hengest. And I will show my friendship towards you with great gifts, such as are given only between men who hold each other dear.'

So it was settled, and Folcwald held a great feast and summoned his wisest rune-scribes to set the terms of our treaty down in letters. We presented Folcwald with all the gifts we had brought, and the minstrel sang a new song in the hall celebrating our journey, and the new friendship of our two peoples.

Finn was as good as his word. When the feasting was at its height he brought out of the secret treasure hoard of the Frisians a gift so splendid that I have never heard of another such being given or received by any man living. First there was a shirt of ring-mail, each ring made of tempered iron, and riveted with bronze, so that the shirt glistened black with a shimmer of gold, like the skin of some fabulous dragon. And with it was the shield I had been promised – this too of a strange shape, long and oblong, and slightly curved round the body. It was ornamented with scrolls, and a boss of gold. Even among kings such armour would be magnificent. I stood amazed to see them laid before me.

Folcwald spoke. 'These things, O Hengest, have lain long ages in our hoard. Long ago when the Roman king needed the help of our fighting men he sent these things to a king of the Frisians long since dead. Time has not perished the workmanship of cunning craftsmen, who knew secret ways of making things which none now knows.'

I looked long at the splendid Roman work, at arms which would make me rich and famous in my own lands, and I thanked Finn with a grateful heart. But that was not all he gave.

'You are a thane to prince Hnaef,' he said, 'and so a share of anything I give you is due to him. It would be a shame to part this shirt and shield which have belonged together for so long. So I will give you this to offer to Hnaef, as his share.' And he gave me also a sword, a splendid weapon, with a blade patterned with snake markings, and a ring upon the pommel. This too was old, and of great worth, though not made in the land of the Romans, but by the Frisians of other days. And the name of the sword was Hunlafing.

Thus were we honoured in the halls of the Frisians until we had to depart. They put us on board one of their great ships, though we were loth to go, not being sailors, and the weather being rough with the storms of spring. But Finn laughed and said he would come with us to show us that he thought it safe. The rest of the party were sea-sick all the way, but I recovered after the first few hours, and though the ship pitched most horribly on the tall waves, I managed to take a good look at her.

At last we grounded on the beaches of our own land. When he had seen us and all our belongings safely ashore, Finn bade me farewell with the fondness of a brother, and climbed back on board his ship. I watched him going until the sail dipped out of sight. It was long before I saw him again.

Chapter Three

How dull and wearisome Hoc's court seemed now! The great hall was bare and smoky, our wooden dishes poor stuff, even our beer no drink to compare with the wine of Frisia. King Hoc seemed greyer and frailer, talking always about the past, his words making less sense with every day which passed. Even my father seemed older and more bent than when we set out. And the young thanes lounged around, and drank and swore and played dice, winning and losing their weapons every day. Defeat had sapped our courage and self-respect. Even the celebration to greet our safe return, and our good news, seemed rough and unruly to me.

The only person I was glad to see again was my cousin Gefwulf. And he was glad enough to see me, for we two had been always together before the journey, and he had been missing my company. But I talked of nothing but the Frisians, and of Finn, so that he grew weary of hearing me, and raged at the fate which kept him at home. Indeed the court of Hoc was a poor place for a young man now. He was jealous of me, and longed to set out on a journey of his own.

One day when time was heavy on our hands I took him down to the underground chamber dug out below our house where I had placed my gifts from Finn for safe keeping, for I thought best not to show them to everyone till the time came to use them. I unlocked the lid of the chest, and lifted them out. When I lifted the ring-

shirt it murmured to me with a faint metallic whisper as the rings slipped against one another. Gefwulf stood holding the torch which gave our only light, envy and admiration on his face. But he mocked at the shield.

'It's the wrong shape!' he said. Then he picked it up and held it. It curved round his body, protecting his sides, as well as his chest, and it covered him from shoulder to knee. 'Hmm,' he muttered. 'But it will not take knocking.' And before I could stop him, he had dropped the shield, and drawn his sword. He raised it above his head, and brought it down upon the shield with all his strength. The clang of the blow rang loudly in the small space. The shield jumped at the blow and I cried out in dismay. But when I picked it up there was a wide band of scratching on the boss where the burnish had been scoured off by Gefwulf's blade, but that was all – there was neither dent nor split in it. And Gefwulf stood looking in consternation

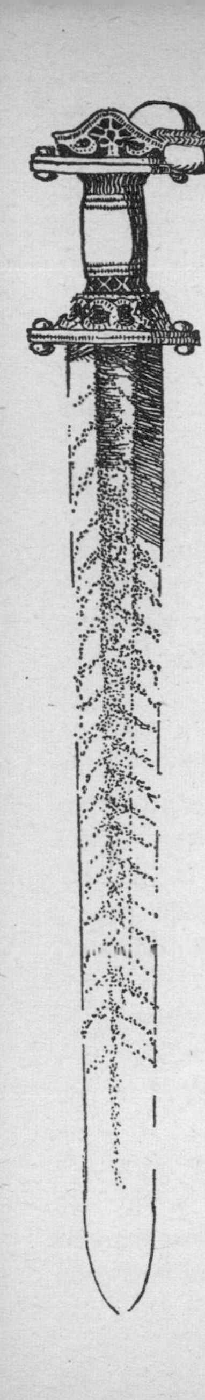

at the blade of his sword which had been cracked by the blow.

I feared he would fly into one of his rages, but he was silent, and fell into a black sullen mood. When I showed him the sword Hunlafing he observed sourly that it was the best of the gifts.

I had not let myself like that cursed sword because it had not been given to me for myself. But it was beautiful. It was handsomely adorned, but it was more than this; the way in which the hilt and blade were balanced made it feel light and agile in my hand, so that one did not doubt that the cut it made would be swift and deadly. I picked it up, and the lust of battle swelled in my heart. And then, in case I should grieve when I had to give it away, I hastily laid it down again. Would that it had never come into my hands; would that I had given Hnaef both the other gifts and left Hunlafing lying harmlessly in Finn's treasury! But I laughed then at Gefwulf's sourness, and climbed back into the light, telling him that it was the dark air we breathed underground which made him ill-spoken.

'By our father Woden!' he said when we walked in the open again, 'I want armour such as that! I want it, and I must have it. I shall grind my teeth down to my jawbone with rage cooped up here, owning nothing of beauty or power. Where is armour such as that to be had?'

'In the lands ruled by the Roman king. From him came these of mine.'

'And how shall a man get there? The Saxons, the vile Danes, and your precious Frisians all have ships, and cross seas and oceans for the wealth, and we sit dully on land, and our feeble boats cannot even keep us in touch with the folk of our own islands when the weather is poor. What fools we are!'

'I think I know what is wrong with our boats,' I said. 'They are too narrow.'

'I suppose you would like to set sail in a nice wide barge like a fisherman!' said Gefwulf sarcastically.

'No, listen Gefwulf, I am not talking lightly. I looked well at the Frisian ship which brought us home, and it is much wider in the beam than ours. So when the water rolls under it, it does not tilt and ship water as ours would do, until they floundered, but keeps on an even keel, and rides the waves.'

Gefwulf was thinking hard. 'But if one built a ship long enough to carry a sea-faring crew, and made it wider, the planks would break and split under the extra-weight.'

'Yet I say the Frisian shipbuilders can do it; and though I will wear my tongue out praising their beauty and wealth, I would scarcely claim that the timber of their forests is stronger than that of ours.'

Then Gefwulf said, 'Did you look well enough at that ship, Hengest, to help me build one like it?'

'I think so. It was so that I could copy that I looked so closely.'

'Praise the gods!' cried Gefwulf, leaping ahead. 'I shall have a real ship, and I shall go and terrify the Romans and take from them armour and weapons and silver and gold, and I shall return here rich and honoured and be famous till I die!'

'Not so fast, Gefwulf,' I said laughing, 'it was for myself that I meant to build this ship.'

'It will be easier for two of us,' he replied. 'Let us work together, and gamble when it is finished. The winner shall take it for his own.'

It was like Gefwulf to let his hopes depend upon a freak of chance; I am not a man to refuse a wager. So began the making of Gefwulf's ship.

I doubt if we would ever have begun it if we had known how hard it would be. Gefwulf got together a group of shipwrights, but they constantly grumbled and disobeyed my instructions, because they were sure the ship would split if we made her wider than usual. In the end we had to do most of the work ourselves, bringing in carpenters to help our unpractised hands here and there, but never letting any one of them work on his own. The men talked of course, and soon we were the object of constant mockery, and everyone who knew, or thought they knew anything about any kind of ship from warship to coracle came down to the shore to gaze at the ribs and keel we had set up, and tell us of the death by drowning which certainly awaited us. But I stuck to my plan; if Finn's ship had not come to pieces ours should be all right. When we were making the ribs I was quite sure of myself; I knew well those of Finn's ship had been broad, rising in a wide curve from the keel, and I made ours likewise. I had seen too that the keel was not just a thick plank, but a stout and solid piece of wood, nearly the girth of a grown man. For our keel we used the trunk of a fine tall oak tree, carefully planed to shape. We made it deep, going well below the level of the bottom, so that it would hold the ship on course against a side wind. Of all this I was quite sure, and I became daily more scornful of the words of those who mocked us; they had even started to say that our keel was so heavy it would drag the ship down and sink her – as if anyone ever saw an oak tree sink!

All this was well enough; but when it came to details I was not so certain. There were many things I should have taken note of which I had not thought of at the time. For instance I knew that the planking of the sides had been lashed to the ribs; but I could not remember how many lashings there had been for each plank, nor had I noticed what the lashings had been made of. We settled for one lashing on each row of planking, and used the finest and toughest sealskin rope, but I was secretly afraid that I would get some small thing wrong, which would be enough to send the ship to the bottom. My worry was exacerbated by the stream of gloomy prophecy uttered by the old man who worked on the stem post at the prow, carving it into a fine dragon's head. We kept him at work because of his skill; but he tried our patience sorely with his constant telling us that we were mad, and making a doomed vessel.

I took to rising early, and reaching the ship before any of our workmen, so that I could see how things went. As time went on, and the ship took shape I started to love her. What an elegant line we had given her! She looked like a sea-bird with wings folded, and I hoped she would ride as sweetly on the waves. I dreamed of sailing her to a land far away where fame and wealth could be won, or of using her for the voyage I had soon to make. For I owed Hnaef his share of my gifts from Finn, and so I would have to go to visit him in Denmark. How splendid it would be if I could arrive in my own ship! This was the only thought which could lighten my dislike for such a journey. I had no wish to go among the Danes.

It was on one of these mornings when I rode before dawn and went out towards the shore, that I found Hildeburg waiting for me at the door of the king's bower. She was wrapped in a dark cloak to keep her from the morning cold, and against it her face showed pale, and her gold hair still unbraided escaped the folds of cloth round her face, and drifted lightly on the breeze of dawn.

'Hengest,' she said, 'I beg you to tell me truly, what sort of man is Finn?' The misery in her voice struck me deeply, for I had not thought much about her feelings. Yet how frightening it must be to go to a stranger in an unknown land, knowing nothing save that one would never see one's own land again! I stood awkwardly for a moment, not knowing what to say, when words would be of such power to help or harm; winged as words always are, they are never to be unsaid, least of all when they go to the heart of a young girl. Then I took her hand and said, 'Finn is brave and honest, generous to all, and in all ways such a man as I would like to serve; you need not fear him.'

'Does he take me only for my dowry?' she asked. How unreasoning women are! Finn had not seen her; for what else could he want her? I could not tell her that my own words had moved him.

'When he knows you, he will want you for yourself,' I said. 'He is a man who appreciates virtue.'

'You mean he thought well of you, Hengest!' she said, laughing. 'What does he look like? Is he tall? Is he young?'

Now I laughed too. 'He is as handsome as the sun,' I told her. 'His hair is like flame, his eyes are like the morning mist, he is tall and he is young.'

'I hope you do not speak to deceive me with false hopes, Hengest,' she said. 'I hope he is all you say.'

'He is all this and more,' I assured her. 'Indeed I wish that I were such a man as he is!'

I left her looking more cheerful, though thoughtful still.

She left for Dorestead a few days later, with a wedding party to escort her, but it was not thought tactful for me to be among them.

So I stayed and the ship made progress. When we came to make the sides we found we had been too ambitious; we could not find anywhere a tree tall and straight enough to make the bulwark in one piece. But of all the parts of the ship this had to be the strongest. For days we rode the forests, talking to woodmen, and searching for a tree; all in vain.

So in the end we made joints in the bulwark plank. We fixed the joints with stout wooden pegs, and caulked them well, but my heart misgave me, for I thought we had built her flawed in this way at least, and I did not trust her.

But Gefwulf was not downcast in the least. He spent the whole of his days down on the shore, always either working or watching like a hawk while others worked. He talked of nothing but the ship, and he trusted me completely, asking question after question about the Frisian ship, and putting every detail I could remember into practice. His energy came from the depth of his longing to voyage in the ship, but he never talked of this, only of the details of the work. He was haunted by his dream voyage, but he kept his thoughts to himself. I knew later how dangerous was Gefwulf's brooding heart; at the time I was full of admiration for his energy, and his refusal to be daunted by difficulty.

At last we finished. The ship carried a small sail, and fifteen pairs of oars, and we bribed our carpenters with offers of lavish payment to launch her, and row her a little way up and down the coast, on a clear calm day when the sea was scarcely puckered by the wind. She swam like the sea-birds who drift easily and ride lightly on the billows of the pathless sea; she was easy to steer, and a joy to ride in;

but all her oarsmen were terrified, and among the crowd who had gathered on the beaches to watch there were no kind words for her even when she was safely beached, and Gefwulf and I came ashore triumphantly.

We both drank deeply in the hall that night, and then we cleared the trestles and benches from the centre of the hall and prepared our game of chance.

We set up a pole as a target, and a little way from it we set up a spear-head, and on the point of the spear we set

an arrow, with a little hollow bored in its shaft, so that it balanced on the point of the spear, and turned at the lightest touch. Then Gefwulf stepped forward and set the arrow spinning. All stood silent while it slowly came to rest. It pointed nearly straight at the target. Now it was my turn, and I set it spinning and watched. I had given it a harder push than Gefwulf, and it seemed to take an age to slow down. It seemed about to stop in a winning position, but so slowly that I could have sworn at every moment it had stopped, it crept past the target post, and was still at last pointing in the other direction. Gefwulf let out a shout of joy, I a groan of disappointment. But as it happened I could not have sailed the ship had I won it, for my father fell ill that very evening and I could not leave his bedside.

While I sat watching the fever sap my father's strength, Gefwulf set about trying to raise a crew for his ship. He announced that he was taking her on a raid on Britain. All the near coasts of that island were well defended, but he had heard from a sailor who had been on a voyage in a Saxon vessel that it was possible to sail right round Britain to the north, though the seas were stormy and the coasts rocky, and on the far side the island was unfortified, and the rich plunder of a Roman province could be had for little fighting.

But what with the evil reputation our efforts at shipbuilding had got, and our people's poor ability as sailors, and the wild sound of Gefwulf's proposed voyage, nobody could be got to go with him. Even the thanes of Hoc's court, even the men returning from the wedding party, who like me were full of the glory of Frisian ways and weary of their own land, were not willing to risk their lives on such an enterprise. Gefwulf gathered his thirty men in the end, but there was not a good man among them, save perhaps himself; they were all the wildest youngsters of the court, all in debt, or fleeing from some crime due for vengeance, or too light-headed to weigh the risk they took, and therefore too light-headed to trust. And above all this none of them knew how to steer, or handle a sail, and Gefwulf's talkative Saxon friend had to take them for lessons in the bay before they could set out.

Even Hoc was distressed. I do not suppose he could have much minded the loss of the dregs of his court; but the sons of some of his oldest and most loyal thanes were among the crew, and Gefwulf himself was a near relation of the king, coming from a line of princes, and the son of Hoc's treasurer.

He spoke to Gefwulf in private, but he failed to stop him. He had always relied on my father's tongue when there was persuasion to be done, and my father lay silent now. Gefwulf announced the day of his departure.

I still remember how my heart sank when I woke that day to the sound of the wind on the eaves, and rising saw the tossing waves. But Gefwulf had said he would go that day, and go he did. I left my father for the first time for days and took a bundle of gifts for Gefwulf down to the shore, where a crowd had gathered, and the ship was in a bustle of final preparations. I had brought a sword, a good one from my father's store to replace the one Gefwulf had broken on my shield, and two skins of wine from the few we had brought from Dorestead, and a jar of salt.

Gefwulf was in a high-wrought mood, and I realized for the first time that he himself did not think his chances of returning alive very great, for he thanked me with tears in his eyes, and taking my hands leaned his head for a moment on my shoulder, as though he thought never to see me again.

I stood on the beach and watched anxiously as the ship was at last launched and breached the first waves. She dipped and rose with the heavy swell, and we saw the white crests of the hostile waves crash against her prow. The oars swept raggedly in the rough water, and she drew away only slowly. Then her sail crept up her mast, and we saw men on deck making fast the ropes. As the sail caught the wind it seemed to me the ship stood still, and shuddered from stem to stern. Then she cut a straight path through the waves, making away westwards like a bird in flight, till my straining eyes could follow her no more. I had no hope for her desperate voyagers, yet I was proud to see her go so swiftly and gracefully.

When I reached home my father was worse. He lay talking feverishly, and now his thoughts were of Hnaef.

'The prince, the prince . . .' he was saying as he tossed on his bed. 'The hope of the nation or its doom . . . alone, and young in an alien land . . . Hengest must go, Hengest must go to him, he needs friends, he needs his thanes, there is that sword to take . . .'

'Hush now, do not fear Father, I will go,' I said.

'Good,' he murmured, and turned over to sleep. It was a sleep which turned to death before evening, without my knowing at what moment it happened.

Hoc plunged his court into mourning for him, and held a great burial feast, with a barrow raised above his grave, but his grief seemed more than ceremonial. He came no more to the feasting in his hall, but sat alone in his chamber, and he held no more councils, so that things went on from day to day without reason or order, and it was only when he was dead that I saw how great my father had been in the kingdom, and how closely Hoc had leaned on his advice.

I did not stay to see this for long. As soon as my father's barrow was finished I assembled horses and provisions, got permission from Hoc, who scarcely seemed to know me, and found myself a guide. Then I went down to the treasure room, and took out my great chest. I got into the ring-shirt, surprised at the weight of it, then pleased at the look of it. Then I picked up my shield, and marched out to the waiting horses.

The thanes who had gathered to see my going greeted my strange and splendid appearance with shouts of admiration. And indeed I felt like a king in my heavy array.

'It will gladden Hnaef's heart, and raise his honour in all men's eyes, when it is seen he has a thane such as that!' said someone.

And this was the thought uppermost in my mind, as I rode like a king going to battle on my way into the land of the Danes.

Chapter Four

Sigehere, king of the Danes, lord of the northern seas, kept his court on one of the islands from which his wealth was drawn. Strong in defence, rich in pasture, their beaches loaded with amber washed up by the sea, the Danish islands were strung out across the narrow seas, holding the trade routes from the far north, whence came slaves and furs and the white ivory from the tusks of walrus, and the far south, where the vassals of the Roman king lived in wealth, and traded wine, and fine weapons in exchange for the goods of the far north.

We had no difficulty in reaching the islands for the land was peaceful, and the fisherfolk were willing to ferry us across. I had followed my father's example, and taken few companions, and I travelled with a great cloak over my ring-shirt, not wanting to draw attention to myself, and risk attack by thieves.

It was the middle of a fine afternoon when we came in sight of Sigehere's hall. We drew up, and gazed down at it in the valley below us. It stood behind a strong earth wall, and it was large with many buildings and stables around it, and gables carved into the writhing shapes of worms and monsters. Behind it rose a hill, steep at first, and then flatter, covered with heather and broom. Smoke drifted in the still air from the vents in the roof. We could see no one moving, and we rode down to it without seeing anyone on the wayside, or in the fields.

The gates stood open and unguarded, and indeed the

power of Sigehere was so great, and so far spread, that there could be no danger against which to guard his walls. But when we entered the gates, and saw still no sign of movement anywhere we were surprised into fear. The stables were full of fine horses, but no grooms attended them; kettles hung in the flames of the fires outside the doors, but no cooks watched them; the only sound was the stamping of hooves, and the scratching of fowl in a yard.

We went up to the door of the hall, hearing only the noise of our horses resounding with unnatural loudness in the silence. We tethered them, and went in, my companions shrinking back to let me enter first, reluctant to follow. In the dark hall the fires had burnt low, and I blinked for a second. The hall too was deserted, or so I thought while my eyes got used to the light. Then I saw, sitting at the far end on one of the mead-benches, a solitary man. He sat slouched in boredom, and his face, that of a youth whose new beard was still soft, was clouded and sullen. He did not look up.

I walked down the hall towards him. The silence was so great I could hear the silken tinkle of the rings of mail upon me with each step I took. As my footfall approached him the young man raised his sulky face to mine, and then with a cry leapt to his feet.

'Hengest!' he said, and clasped my hands in his.

At that I recognized Hnaef, and went down on my knees before him. Then I stood, and threw back my cloak, and beckoned to my page to bring the sword Hunlafing. Hnaef stood and gazed at me, and I at him. The new beard on his chin, and the new height he had grown to since I saw him last had changed him from a boy into a man; I was no longer the thane of a mere child. For my part I knew my value, as I stood before him, a fighting man in the prime of youth, armed with a splendour fit for a king, and bringing gifts of great price to lay at the feet of my lord. I knew my value to an untried prince, and I wanted no more of Hnaef than that he should know it too. I laid Hunlafing in his lap, looking down proudly at him as I stooped to do so.

He undid the fine linen, and saw the sword lying in its jewelled sheath. The gems glittered dimly, the wrought snakes twined around the hilt before our eyes. The ring on the pommel gleamed brightly. Hnaef looked long at it, and then he looked up at me, his eyes bright from the joy it gave him. And then he leapt to his feet, and cried out,

'Come, Hengest, come, we shall make use of this gift at once. I shall not after all have no fine offering to lay my hands on. I shall not be called Hnaef Bystander after all! Come now, or we shall be too late!' And he seized his cloak, and brandishing Hunlafing over his head, he ran from the hall.

I followed him. He did not wait to saddle a horse, but leapt on to the first one in the nearest stable. I too mounted, and we galloped out of the town gate. Up the hill on the far side of the town we went, galloping along a track leading over the hill. It was narrow and overgrown, but it had recently been used by many people; the bracken on either side was trodden down by many feet, small branches were broken, and deep drag marks were scored in the turf, as though heavy things had been laboriously drawn up the hillside. Along this track we rode for some distance, while it wound around, climbing slowly towards the hilltop. And then as we got nearer the point where the path disappeared over the crest I heard a strange noise. It grew louder as we rode towards it, till it was a clamorous din, above which I could not hear the hooves of the horse I rode on, and above which Hnaef did not hear my shouted questions.

It was the sound of many voices, raised and shouting, and mingled with horrible screams either animal or human, and a clanging and crashing like a thousand smiths battering their ironwork at once. In that lonely and deserted place it was frightening; it seemed to me that Hnaef was riding headlong into the midst of a den of ogres. And then we came over the crest and I saw what it was.

Below us in a hollow between the spur we had just climbed and the next, lay a small mountain lake, the water brown with the hillside peat, and glossy in the clear light of early evening. And round the shore of this lake there surged a great mob of Danish soldiers, and all the men of Sigehere's court. Around the water's edge in unbelievable chaos lay piles of armour and clothing, and packs of equipment of all kinds, great heaps of silver and gold vessels, bundles of swords and spears, and a row of large ships, six of them great sea-faring vessels, which must have taken days to heave up the hill. Hundreds of horses were tethered to stakes, and next to them stood a group of slaves, bound together. In all my long life I have never seen so strange a scene. Before us lay collected unthinkable wealth – the booty of a great victory over a richly furnished army; and the victorious Danes were swarming round it, shouting and crying, and working to destroy it. Here a group of men were smashing shields and helmets with great hammers, here men were hacking chain mail to bits with axes, and blunting and bending swords and spears. A little way off frenzied men were slaughtering horses, and not content to kill them were hacking the carcases to pieces, and to our right yet more screaming men were dragging the bodies of hanged captives down to the water's edge. Even the children were busy breaking up clay jars and dishes.

I was terrified. I thought the entire nation of the Danes had been seized by an evil spirit, and all gone berserk at once. But Hnaef rode straight down into the milling throng, and disappeared among them. I sat there on my horse, stunned into inaction. While I watched, people were dragging the shattered goods, and loading them into the ships. The two ships nearest me were already filled to the gunwhales with gleaming fragments of armour, and ragged chunks of butchered horse-flesh. I saw a trickle of blood running down the planks from the rowlocks. On top of this gruesome cargo men were now laying the corpses of the slaughtered slaves. The noise was shattering. But slowly through my dumbfounded mind there came the realization of what Hnaef had meant: 'I shall have something to offer – '

He was going to take my gift, the thing of priceless worth, and heart-catching beauty I had brought him, the gift I had won from Finn out of the strength of friendship, and he was going to smash it in that fearful frenzy of senseless waste which raged before my eyes. With a cry of dismay I slipped from my saddle and followed him.

I ran through the crowd. I did not stop to look, but I remember, even after all this time, seeing the dark rage on hundreds of faces at which I scarcely glanced. Here a man lifted a spear high above his head, and drove it down with great force so that it pierced through a pile of fine shields pinning them together, and twisting its point in the ground. Here a man hacked at a fine shirt of leather and mail, carefully reducing it to small square fragments a few inches across. Here a man ran across my path, carrying towards the ships a bundle of broken weapons.

I found Hnaef standing among the courtiers beside the biggest ship, with Hunlafing in one hand, held across an anvil, and a hammer in the other hand. He raised the hammer to bring it down on the blade, and swirled it above his head. As he did so someone pointed upwards to the ship. One of the bodies of the hanged had risen to its feet. The man stood with the rope still round his neck, his face twisted in a cry that could not be heard above the surrounding din. I suppose the poor devil had decided to avenge his own death, for he stood there ready to jump, with a huge broken whetstone in his raised hand. He stood swaying for a second, and then leapt down, and made straight for Hnaef, with his murderous stone held high. Hnaef turned round just in time, ducked swiftly under the blow, missing the stone by a hair's breadth, and with the ease which comes from practice at swordplay he gave the wretch a merciful death with a single blow of Hunlafing. Then he let the hammer drop and slid the sword back into its splendid sheath. I could see on his face the battle lust which the sword had put into my heart when I held it. It had been blooded in Hnaef's hands, and once having felt its grace and power he could not bear to break it. How glad I was! How I rejoiced to see him keep it! And how often since have I wished that he had given it to the dark goddess of the brown lake, and left it where it would never more have tasted blood!

We stood and watched while all the ships were loaded. The last of the broken things were laid on the decks, and now men brought stones, and wildly battered the planks of the ships' sides, tearing great holes in them. When all the ships were loaded a priest came down to the shore and spoke loudly to the lake-goddess, telling her that the booty was hers in exchange for the victory she had given, and asking her to grant victory again, that she might be still more generously paid.

And then sails were hoisted, shoulders were put to the stern posts, and the ships were pushed out into the lake. There was a strong cold wind blowing, in the dusk, and a red sunset smouldering in the west. The ships slid rapidly out over the puckered waters, crashed one against the other as they went rudderless before the wind, and then sank. Each went down differently. One was simply sucked down, with a loud gurgle of water, one tipped over sideways, spilling its load into the lake, and lying with its sail spread out on the water for several minutes before going under. One went down stern first, its carved prow tilting like some animal trying to keep its head above water till the last.

When the last ship disappeared a low sigh rose from the crowd. Not a word was spoken, no cry of triumph arose. The Danes simply turned round and started to file down the homeward path. They went slowly, their feet dragging, their shoulders sagging, their arms hanging lifelessly by their sides like a procession of the dead. They had been three days and nights at their task, and they were exhausted.

No moon came out to light them down. We went in darkness in a cold still night, in which the sound of muffled, shuffling footfalls whispered all around us. Hnaef and I rode together, our horses picking their way over the bodies of men who had dropped down on the wet hillside to sleep where they lay. Hnaef was friendly and cheerful, and asked questions about home, but I answered with only scant attention. I was thinking gloomily of the beauty and usefulness of the things I had seen destroyed, of the different ways of the Frisians, who cherished wealth and beauty, and lived in grace and luxury, and of these hard northern men who smashed things and lived only for power and fighting, in a hall bare of finery – lacking indeed everything that the Frisians would think fitting for a great king, except the band of brave thanes. Of those there was no denying the Danish king had plenty.

'I tire you with questions, Hengest,' said Hnaef at last. 'You have journeyed today, and you are weary. I will find you a warm place to make your bed tonight. Only tell me of my sister – what news is there of her since she was forced to marry the enemy prince?'

'She is well,' I said. 'But the Frisians are not enemies of ours, even if they are enemies of the Danes.'

'They are not enemies of the Danes as yet,' said Hnaef, 'but it would come to the same thing.' But I was too tired to be alarmed at what he said.

We came at last to the great hall, finding the fires burnt out, and the place cold and dark. A few torches were lit, a few bundles of rushes were brought in, but most of the company lay down on the bare floor and slept like the dead. Hnaef and I lay side by side, I in little comfort, for I slept in my ring-shirt, being unwilling to lay it by in a strange place. And between us lay Hunlafing.

It was early dawn when the messengers arrived. They came galloping up in a grey light, grey themselves with dust from head to foot, their sweating horses near to dropping. We woke to a great cry in the hall.

'Hnaef, prince of the Jutes, where is he?'

'Here,' said Hnaef, standing, and rubbing the sleep from his eyes.

'The king your father is dead,' said the newcomer, the words slow and leaden with the weariness of the speaker. 'Hoc is dead, and if his son is to hold his place in the kingdom he must come home at once. Mount and ride with us, son of Hoc!'

Someone went and brought Sigehere himself to the hall. He listened to the news in silence, his stern face expressionless and cold. Then he asked questions. Hoc's undisciplined thanes were rioting and fighting among themselves, and dividing the land.

'Hnaef must go,' said Sigehere. 'And he must have men with him he can trust to help him take and rule his own.'

'Here at my side is my thane Hengest,' said Hnaef, 'who of all men is most worthy of my trust.'

Sigehere looked hard at me. He did not mean Hnaef to have companions unknown to him.

'I will give you two of my most faithful thanes,' he said to Hnaef, 'with all their men. Reward their service well, and you will thus repay me for my hospitality.'

The men he chose were two brothers, called Guthlaf and Oslaf. They came heavy-eyed from sleep, and in front of their lord they knelt to Hnaef, and gave him their allegiance. All round us in the gloom their friends slept on, unawakened by the sound of oath-taking. These two were tall fierce men, with proud bearing and battle-scarred faces. It seemed to me that they were stronger than their new master, and little likely to forget their old one.

'Let me go too, Sigehere,' said a voice from behind me. 'I am best where there is fighting to be done.'

Sigehere considered. 'Go,' he said.

So we rode from his court, Hnaef, and Guthlaf and Oslaf and I, and several hundred men, and with us came Sigeferth, prince of the Secgan, who was also a hostage of the Danes.

We rode hard, and in my weariness I did not know whether I felt more relief at leaving the court of the Danes, or fear of the trouble which lay ahead.

Chapter Five

Trouble did meet us when we reached home. Some of the Jutes were out to seize what they could and increase their wealth and power in the ruin of the land; some wished only to take advantage of the leaderless time to settle old scores; more would not accept a king who came surrounded by friends and advisers from the hated nation of the Danes. Few indeed remembered the oath they had sworn to Hnaef when Hoc was still alive. The fighting was harsh, and it grieved me, for the men we fought were my hall-companions of the old days, and men of my own stock. Naturally such thoughts did not worry the Danes, and Hnaef had become so much one of them that he did not care either, but fought for his own interest without scruple.

The fiercest opposition to Hnaef came from a young thane called Horsa, whose father had fallen in the great battle against the Danes. Horsa gathered bold men around him, and held out in the hills all winter, so that it took us as long to drive him out, as to win the whole of the rest of the land. At last he was beaten, and he fled, taking his men, and going westwards towards Frisia.

Yet it was only now, when the land was peaceful again that the trouble really began. Hnaef took as his councillors all the Danes of noble blood who had fought with him, and only me from the Jutes. When it came to giving rewards for the services of his warriors, Hnaef was more generous to the Danes than was wise. He took all the lands of the defeated rebels and gave them to his Danish followers. To me he gave the lands and the place on his council which were my father's as mine by right. But to Oslaf and Guthlaf he offered the choice of anything he had to give, for their service had been of great worth.

Indeed they had done well. They had fought like wolves without fear, and without weariness; they cared for little except battle, taking pleasure in drinking deeply, and taking pride only in loyalty to their lord. They were dull company at table, but good thanes to Hnaef.

A week after Hnaef had made his offer to the two brothers they came to him in council, and asked for the lands which had belonged to his father's treasurer to be shared between them, and the position and honour of the post to be given to Oslaf who was the elder.

'The treasurer is dead, I know,' said Hnaef, 'but he has an heir, and the honour has always been handed from father to son since men can remember. Gefwulf was the son's name. Where is he now?'

'He set sail in an unseaworthy ship, going on a voyage of great danger round the coasts of Britain, nearly two years ago, and he has not been heard of since. His lands lie empty and we ask for them.'

'But if he is not dead, they are not yours to give,' I said to Hnaef.

'Surely he is dead!' said Hnaef, 'and I will not refuse my thanes what they ask, since I said they should have anything they would.' So he gave Gefwulf's land and title to the two Danes. Indeed when it came to the giving of gifts he was always more generous to the Danes than to the Jutes in his service. And there were many who sat and watched him who remembered the bitter defeat which had led to his exile. If he had forgotten all bitterness, and felt only gratitude to his captors, these others had not forgotten.

So it was an uneasy peace we won, even when the fighting was over. Quarrels broke out in Hnaef's hall; they grew more bitter, and they happened more often as time went by, and the Jutes saw themselves passed over, and realized that the blood that had been shed to keep us from being slaves of the Danes had been shed in vain, for our own king was their willing servant. As soon as the drink flowed, insults were shouted, and men imagined that they could see in the hands of a Dane across the table, some weapon stripped from a dead father or brother after the great battle. Hnaef took from the Danes all their weapons, and gave them new ones, but it was idle to quell one cause of trouble without soothing the sore feelings behind it.

Loaded with wealth and honour the Danes did not conceal their contempt for the Jutes whom they had conquered; and among the Jutes there rose a murmured taunt, passed round in whispers at first, and then spoken openly. Hnaef, the word went, Hnaef the Half-Dane, lord of the Half-Danes, and master of the Jutes. But Hnaef when he heard it was not angry, but laughed and said, 'That is praise indeed.'

So the ill feeling festered, until at last blood was shed. There was shouting between men sitting at the bottom of the hall, then a sudden scuffle, and a cry, and when the fighters were dragged apart by their friends a young Jute of high birth lay bleeding across the bench, wounded to his death.

And now the doom-laden feud was too far gone to be stopped. Hnaef it is true, found and killed the man he said was the murderer; but the man he blamed was a Jute, and nobody but the Danes believed that the killer of a Jute could have been any but a Dane. One after another many of Hnaef's Jutish thanes, even those who had accepted him willingly at first, slipped away and deserted him, with hatred and resentment in their hearts. After the murder in the hall they went in dozens.

Where could they go? They always went west. They went to Frisia, where there was a Jutish princess to hear their story and take pity on them, as long as they did not blame her brother, but only his Danish men. And there was also a chance to take service with the Frisian prince; for he was looking for men to go with him to his new stronghold in the north of the land. Where could they go? They went to Finn. And Finn gave them work to do.

We heard tell of Finn's doings; of the hall he had built and the town near a good anchorage; of the travels of his ships and the success of his trade. His town became famous far and wide. It did not equal Dorestead, but he was a prince, not yet a king, and for a prince men said there was none to outshine him, even in the tales of the heroes of old. His fame drew men to serve him, and especially the exiled and the desperate. I thought much about this. It did not seem good to me that Hnaef's enemies should all gather in one place – and it seemed worse that that place should be the home of his sister.

Another winter came in, and the weather was strange, wet and cool, and wreathed in thick white fog, which drifted for days and never lifted. We were reduced to eating only salt meat for the fisherfolk could not take their boats out for fear of losing their way in the featureless haze. For more than a month the fog continued, and there was no wind to blow it away. Everything was wet and clammy, and we stayed miserably indoors, huddled round our fires, talking idly. Then one afternoon Oslaf came in, and announced that there was a ghost ship in the bay, and called on us all to go down and look. Anything was better than sitting in the hall, so a party of us mounted our shivering horses, and groped our way through the blind whiteness to the shore. When we got there there was an excited group of the common folk, standing telling each other what they had just seen, and nothing for us to see at all. We could see only a few yards out to sea, except when a light breeze blew a brief vista in the blank wall of white. We stood straining our eyes and seeing nothing. Once I thought I saw a faint outline as of a ship's hull, but I was looking so hard I could not be sure that it was not only the effort of my eyes shading the fog. But although we saw nothing we talked with the fisherman who had been brave enough to put out to sea a little way, and said he had gone close to the ship and hailed it. He said it had no sail, only rags hanging from the cross-beam. It seemed to be empty, for nobody rowed it, though the oars dragged in the water, lashed to the gunwhale but not manned. And he could see no sign of life aboard her. He had become frightened and put back to shore. Now he was enjoying the attention he commanded as he told everyone about it, and his story got wilder with every repetition. I shrugged my shoulders and went home.

But when we had finished eating that night, and sat listening to the minstrel singing as usual a song about the prowess of the Danes, there was a sound at the door. At first only those nearest heard it, for it was not loud; but gradually the silence travelled down the hall, and reached Hnaef on his chair, and we all sat listening with a chill of fear upon our ale-flushed cheeks. At the door was a faint tapping, which changed as we listened to a scraping noise, as someone struggled to lift the bolt. Sigeferth, who was a man without fear of man or devil, leapt up and unbarred the door. We sat still, frozen in our places, all eyes fixed on the black panel of the outer night, left by the open door. Through it drifted a smoky wisp of fog, and the cold air flowed round our feet while the fires flickered in the draught. And then very slowly, someone came in. With shuffling steps and the slight uncontrolled waver of extreme exhaustion, a ragged man, with starved skin sunken on his bones, and wild hair glistening with droplets from the moist air, came staggering up the hall. And behind him the doorway filled up with figures as terrible as he.

A sigh ran through the hall, but nobody spoke. Nobody rose to welcome him. The ghost captain and his crew had silenced us all. At last he looked up at Hnaef, and said in a loud hoarse voice,

'King Hnaef, your treasurer has come home!'

At this two things happened at once. I ran forward to embrace him, crying out 'Gefwulf!' and Oslaf rose, drawing his sword, and said,

'That title is mine, and I will fight to keep it!'

Gefwulf looked at Oslaf, looked round at us all, bewildered and silent. His lips were crusted with salt from the stinging sea, he was cold and tired, and starving and much had changed since last he stood in this hall.

It was long before he spoke; then, 'Who are you?' he said to Oslaf. And then, 'I have come home.'

There was uproar. From all round the hall the Jutes called out to him. 'Ha! Home, Gefwulf? Where is that?' 'The worms have been at your treasure, Gefwulf, while your back was turned!' 'Ask Hnaef what he has done with your lands, Gefwulf!'

The surge of noise crashed round Gefwulf's tired head. At last it seemed the sense of some of the cries got through to him.

'What has he done with my land?' he asked me.

'He has given it to his Danish lackey!' cried someone.

'Is it true, Hengest?' I nodded, with tears of anger in my eyes.

'Whom shall I kill?' he asked. His anger blazed in him, straightening his drooping limbs, and fired his sunken face to a terrible fury. He looked like a man possessed. And all this while Oslaf stood before him with a drawn sword, and Hnaef did nothing. He did not speak; he did not move to welcome Gefwulf, in whose veins after all the blood of the gods also ran.

Then Oslaf said, 'I am the man whom you must fight!'

Gefwulf fumbled in his ragged cloak, and drew a sword rusted and salty from the sea. Men ran to move the trestles which stood between them, and stood back leaving a space around them.

Desperately I turned to Hnaef.

'You will not let a man who is your kin, who is a prince, who served your father, be set upon while he stands sick and in need before your throne?'

But Gefwulf said, 'He who would not protect me in absence shall not shame me with his protection now.'

And he swung his sword and rushed at Oslaf. Oslaf did not move. He stood planted squarely, and he took Gefwulf's stroke without moving. Gefwulf's sword struck him on the shoulder, but so lightly that it would not have hurt a naked babe. And then Oslaf simply pushed Gefwulf over with the flat of his blade. Gefwulf staggered, so little strength remained to him, and fell to the ground at Oslaf's feet. The scornful tap of Oslaf's blade had felled him.

Once more there was uproar, but this time it was the noise of laughter. The Danes were helpless with mirth, Oslaf stood over Gefwulf, his head thrown back, his huge frame shaking with laughter. Gefwulf slowly raised his head from the dust. He looked through Oslaf's parted

legs and between them he saw Hnaef, sitting in the high-seat of the king, richly robed, and at his ease, and Hnaef too was laughing.

All round Gefwulf, people saw the look upon his face, and the laughter died away. But Hnaef could not see Gefwulf below him; at last his voice only was heard laughing in the hushed hall.

With the noise of the king's laughter ringing in his ears Gefwulf tried to get up. He got to his knees, and then could get no further. I put my arms under his elbows, and lifted him to his feet. He was light as a child in my hands. When I set him upright he stood facing Oslaf, and behind Oslaf, Hnaef. His shame and rage burnt upon his face, and while he looked at them they did not move, or speak, and the laughter died upon their lips.

Then there came from Gefwulf's lips, a faint hoarse voice, scarcely loud enough to hear, and harsh with the effort of speaking.

'Do not forget this night, O Hnaef, thou Half-Dane king, for I shall remember!'

Then he turned, and dragged himself down the hall with slow steps. Every painful step he took could be heard in the silent hall. As he neared the door the Danish party began to shout jibes after him.

'Where is the treasure you were going to win, Gefwulf?' 'How many Roman lands did you lay waste?' 'Where did you take your great ship?' 'Did you win those fine clothes from a defeated enemy, Gefwulf?'

Gefwulf did not answer. He disappeared amidst the wretched ragged shapes of his miserable crew, still standing in the doorway. They melted away into that cruel night, and the darkness and mist closed around them at once. I ran after them, and did not find them. I could not see or hear any trace of them, but wandered around shouting uselessly into the night. At last I went back into the hall, and sat down again in my place. Had I found Gefwulf in the mist, I should never have come back to sit in Hnaef's hall.

For a week I did not speak to him, or to any of the Danes. Then Hnaef came and spoke kind words to me, and melted me with his friendly ways. But when I did speak it was still in anger.

'You have not done well to treat him thus, Hnaef. Though he had not served you, yet he is of princely rank, and he has suffered much. And you are not wise to make yourself an enemy who will hate you as Gefwulf will hate you now.'

Hnaef answered, 'He is a madman who wastes his strength upon such wild journeys; a man without usefulness to me or his people. But I did not like Oslaf's doing. The words to stop him were upon my lips, when Gefwulf refused my help. Would he not also have hated me for his shame if I had protected him against his will? And as for his hatred, do not trouble yourself. They tell me he returned to the shore, and put out to sea again in his storm-battered ship. And on such a night as that, too, when his men had scarce strength to row. His hatred is quenched by now in the remorseless sea!'

'He was my friend,' I said. 'But for your sake I hope that is so.'

And indeed for many years we heard no more of Gefwulf. But he was not dead. His fearless soul had not been conquered by our neglect; nor by the inhospitable sea; nor had our fine ship failed him at the last, having borne him so far.

And so the doom that hung over us was prepared. But still all seemed well, and we lived in peace. From time to time we heard news of Finn; he was our ally, and he had kept the truce his father made with mine, and honoured Hildeburg and loved her. And as the years went on the son of the first year of his marriage was nearing the age at which he could wield a sword. Sooner or later, whatever Hnaef thought of the Frisians, he would have to fulfil his duty towards this boy. The boy was his sister's son, a sacred bond of kinship, and according to the custom of all peoples of the north it was at the court of his uncle that a prince learned the skills of battle and the graces of the hall. Therefore Hnaef had to take the son of Finn and Hildeburg, and bring him home to us, and shelter him and teach him. But the visit which we would have to pay Finn, to fetch the boy, a visit which I had long foreseen and looked forward to, as the one chance life was likely to offer me to see Finn again, and again enjoy the splendour of the Frisian ways, became a less happy-seeming and more dangerous enterprise with every Jute whom we would face again when we got there.

No man can escape the turning years. The seasons come and go, and who can live in the spring, when it is the time for autumn? So in time, whether we liked it or not, the year came in which we had to take the boy, and we sent letters to Finn asking for him. Finn sent a courteous and gracious old man as his messenger, bidding us come and be welcome, and take young Garulf from his hands. Feasts were to be ready for us, and all things that a guest could desire.

'Do not mistrust your welcome,' the messenger told us, 'for Finn has taken a great oath from all the Jutes in his company, that they will keep their feelings in their hearts unspoken, and will strictly keep the peace and gentleness with which he wishes to receive his guests. Only he asks you, as a favour to a friend, that you will take oaths from those you bring, that they will not taunt or anger any of his thanes, nor remind them of old things best forgotten, but will also hold their peace.'

'This is well and wisely done,' said Hnaef. 'All those I bring shall swear to this.' Then he turned to me. 'I shall be glad to see my sister,' he added. 'Will she, I wonder, be glad to see *me*?'

Chapter Six

The land of northern Frisia was low and flat, and at each high tide the sea sent long arms of water over it, so that it was salty and desolate marsh land full of the hard tall grasses which grow in acrid soil, and loud with the cries of wild birds, and empty of men. We would have had trouble finding our way across it in safety if we had been left to ourselves. The land reminded me of the last part of our journey to Dorestead long ago, and my thoughts were much in the past.

And on our third day in Frisia, as I remembered that it was then that we had first seen Finn and his men ride beside our path, we turned a bend in the path through the rushes along which we rode, and saw ahead of us a slender boy, wearing a cloak of deep saffron dye, sitting astride a magnificent horse, and staring at us with a level gaze from pale eyes. His red-gold hair was bound with a fillet of gold, his cloak was fastened with a gem-laden pin, and he sat gracefully at ease, and looked at us without speaking.

I turned to Hnaef, who rode beside me.

'This is Finn's son,' I said. I saw Hnaef glow with pleasure at the fine figure his nephew cut.

'Are you indeed my sister's son?' he asked.

'As to that I do not know,' said the boy, with a twisted smile. 'I am Garulf, son of Finn, son of Folcwald, a prince of this people. Who are you?'

But before we could answer the rest of his party rode

up to us. They were thanes of the court of Finnsburg, and in the midst of them rode Finn himself. How my heart ached to see him! For after long separation even joy is painful. He wore still the long cloak of purple which he used to wear, but now it had a wide border of silver embroidery. His hair was still the colour of copper, and bound with a circlet of gold, but now the hair was threaded with white, and the circlet bore a splendid emerald gleaming on his brow. At the first glance I thought he had not changed, and then at the second I saw he had, for the eager expression of his youth was tempered now with gravity and pride. He had the look, not of a boy with things to do, but of a man with things done behind him. Indeed he and his son looked like a pair of gods.

I remember that Finn greeted us, calling Hnaef brother, and me friend, and telling us how Hildeburg at home counted the hours till she saw her brother and countrymen again. With him at our side the journey was soon and safely finished. We reached Finnsburg by torchlight, after dark, seeing nothing but the clustered lights above us as we came in. A hall was made ready for us, a new one, built for our visit, near the great hall, with a wide yard between them. Inside all was made ready, with fires burning, clean rushes on the floor, new benches set out, and new water jars and cups of red pottery. Great pitchers of ale stood at one end for us to draw from as we pleased; there were hooks to hang up our weapons, and thick woollen blankets to keep us warm at night. A harp stood ready for anyone who felt like singing to his companions. How welcome it all was after the fatigues of the journey!

The good smell of roasting meat wafted across to us from the great hall, and when we had unloaded our packs and washed the dust of the road from our limbs we went across to the evening meal.

Finn's hall was warm and bright. It was scarcely half as big as the one at Dorestead, but it was bigger than Hnaef's own. The walls were kept warm by great hangings of woollen cloth – plain dyed stuff, not tapestry like those of Dorestead – yet taking enough wool to clothe an army; a more costly comfort than we could afford. There were not many women at Finnsburg; but those there were sat at ease among the men, talking gaily and keeping the drinking-horns filled. Among them was Hildeburg, in a dress of white, and a necklet of gold. She rose at once, and taking Hnaef by the hand led him to sit beside her, near Finn's great chair.

Finn's thanes made us welcome, giving us the benches by the fire, and coming to sit among us, and talk of the journey, and exchange names with us. They were as I remembered the men of Dorestead, lacking no skill to grace their daily lives, knowing all the arts of courtesy which put men at their ease.

The hall filled up, as more and more men came in and took their places. And now we began to see faces we knew. They did not meet our eyes, nor take places near us, they took care not to cross paths with us, but they were there. And they were many. When Finn came in, and the red dishes were laden with meat and set before us, I guessed as I looked round me that roughly a third of Finn's thanes were exiled Jutes. In the midst of them, talking and laughing with the ease of friendship sat Garulf. I looked towards him, and the face of the man who sat beside him troubled me. It was a face I knew, but try though I might I could not remember where I had seen it, nor why it alarmed me more than any of the other familiar faces I saw. Soon Hildeburg went down the hall with a jug of wine, and spoke to Garulf as she passed. He rose at once, and came and sat beside Hnaef and opposite me. But he joked and laughed no more, and his face was stony.

When the meal was over Hnaef brought out his gifts. He undid the linen wrapping, and let seven lovely twisted torques fall into his sister's lap in a ringing golden shower. Seven of his thanes, with me the first among them, came up and laid seven drinking-horns at Finn's feet. They were bright with bands of silver set with gems. Then Hnaef unhooked a plain sword from his belt, and gave it to Garulf.

'There is no gold and silver on the hilt of this sword, Nephew,' he said. 'Nor do snakes twine along the blade, nor is it bright with a ring upon the pommel. But it is for a man whose glory is yet to be won; and it is all that such a man needs – it has a strong blade, and a biting edge!'

'I thank you, Uncle,' said Garulf, taking it with his strange dry smile. 'I do not wish to feast my eyes on the hilt of a sword, for I shall hold it in my hand. And little do I care that the sword I carry is not adorned with rings and jewels. For it shall be nobly bedecked with blood!'

At his words there was silence, and uneasiness clouded our faces.

'Minstrel, a song!' cried Finn, swiftly, and the feast went on pleasantly till sleep overcame us, and drew us one by one to bed.

The dawn came pale and bright the next day. Hnaef and I rose early, both wanting to see Finnsburg, and went out into the moist morning air. Nobody stirred in the other hall; a little way off we could hear the sound of a hammer on an anvil which told us that Finn's people worked early. We started across the yard, to walk round the great hall, and down into the main part of the town.

'Good morning to you both!' called a gay voice from the door of Finn's house, which faced on to the yard. 'Where do you go so early?' Finn stood leaning on his doorpost, waiting for us it seemed.

'We go to see the town you have made, Finn,' said Hnaef.

'Let me be your guide, brother,' said Finn gladly. 'I

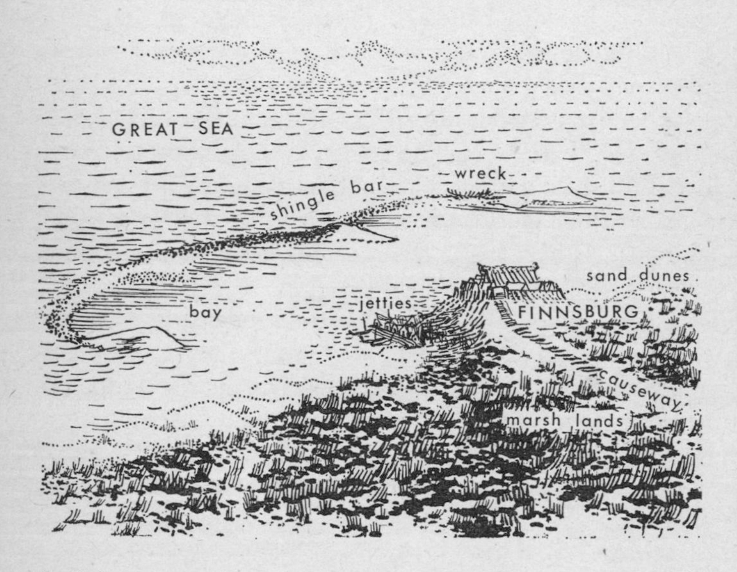

shall be pleased to show you, and Hengest, to whom I once boasted of my plans, what has come of them. Do you remember that talk, Hengest?'

'Indeed yes. We sat in the prow of a fisherboat, sailing home up the great river in the twilight.'

Finn laughed. 'A long memory is a pleasant thing!' he said.

'So it is – between friends,' I answered.

We set off together to see round his little realm.

Finnsburg was built on a low flat-topped mound,

standing among the rolling dunes of a sandy shore. Behind the lines of dunes lay the wide flat marshes, stretching back eastward as far as we could see. Across these a narrow causeway had been built, and it was along this that we had come the night before. On the other side of the dunes was a wide smooth bay, calm as a lake, for it was cut off from the open sea by a great bar of sand and shingle with which the eddying tides had linked up three little off-shore islands. On this wide expanse of wide shallow water three ships rode safely at anchor. At the tip of the southernmost island Finn had set a beacon to guide ships into his splendid harbour. The water sparkled in the clear air; the sky curved high above us. The choppy grey ocean lurched and broke beyond the golden bar. All this we saw from the top of the ramparts round the town, a rough wall built of earth, and faced with timber.

As we walked round the walls Finn told us how the town was run. He had craftsmen and common labourers enough for common needs, he had thanes to keep him company, and to go out in his great ships to escort the traders, and attack pirates if need be. At first there had been much fighting to do, but now the fame of his men had spread widely, and there were few attacks on his ships. Only now and then he had to ward off the Saxons when he had rich cargoes to bring in. The rest of the folk of the town were seamen and merchants, drawn there by love of gain, who traded all down the coasts of Gaul and Spain, and up the coasts of Norway, growing rich and paying a heavy tax into Finn's coffers for the privilege of using Finnsburg, and the protection of his arms.

He had brought to Finnsburg all that was needed for a plain but comfortable life, and he was content there, but his thanes had farms and homes of their own in the south, and duties at the court of Dorestead too. So they spent six months of the year with Finn in the north, and six months free in the south, changing in spring and autumn, so that Finn had half of them with him at a time.

Finn said they would be short of wine, and many other things if they had to rely on what they could make or grow in Finnsburg, but his ships sailed up and down the coast between the mouth of the great river, and the anchorage beneath us, bringing all he needed from the south.

When we walked upon the landward side Finn told us of plans he had to make a great earth wall to hold back the sea from flooding, and dykes to drain the marsh. Then he could farm the land around, and bring in rich harvests to feed his town. Hnaef shook his head, scarce believing such wild talk, but Finn said the Romans had done such things. And he had sent with much gold to a far city called Constantinople, where the Roman king still ruled, to find a cunning craftsman who could carry out such plans. In this he had not changed at all – his head was still full of dreams! Yet in the old days it had been Finnsburg of which he dreamed, and Finnsburg was real enough now.

As the days of the visit went by we became familiar with the life of the town. There was little hunting to do in that marshy and sodden waste, but there was fowling with hidden nets among the grasses, a sport new to us which we learned with eagerness, and hawking, and searching for eggs among the dunes. There was always a bustle going on at the shore, where there were storehouses, and shipbuilding, and much loading and unloading of goods, and a smell of tar and salt in the air. We waited for a chance to set out to sea against pirates, but none came. And we talked and laughed together, and Finn looked smiling at Hildeburg, who walked everywhere with Hnaef, happy to have her family together.

Only Garulf seemed less pleased with it all than the rest of us. One day I went to find him, where he sat as usual, talking among a group of Jutes, for I saw with misgiving how many of them were his friends.

'I have a mind to go across the bay and walk upon the shingle bar, and see Finnsburg from the other side,' I said to him. 'Will you take me, Prince Garulf?'

He glanced quickly up at me, and quickly away. He hesitated, and then he rose and came with me.

We found a small boat, just big enough for two, with a little sail, and launched her from the beach. Garulf was a skilled handler of tiller and ropes, and we went skimming over the water with the foam springing from the prow. He took us to a beach on the northern island, and we went ashore, and climbed to the highest point. Finnsburg seemed surprisingly far away, very flat on its little mound, and not very impressive. I turned away after only a minute's gazing.

'Shall we go back?' asked Garulf.

'Not yet. I want to walk upon the shingle and see the water on my left and on my right.' We went down and walked upon it. The pebbles shifted under foot, and we slipped around, and walked slowly.

'You are not talkative for a young man,' I said.

'What would you have me say?' he asked.

'I would know why it pleases you little to sit with us at the feasting, and why you are cold to your uncle, who has shown only kindness to you.'

'When my uncle goes from here,' said the boy slowly, 'he takes me with him, to serve him till my manhood, according to our custom from of old. When I sit at his table, and eat what he gives, I am bound to see that I am pleasing to him. But until then I am my own master, and I do as I wish. Do you tell me otherwise?'

But I had no wish to quarrel with him.

'What is that? A wrecked ship by the look of it,' I said to change the subject.

We had walked out along the shingle about a quarter of a mile, and I saw half buried in sand and stones, on the seaward side of the bar, the timbers of a vessel bleached and split by salt water, and covered with barnacles, sticking up like the fingers of two hands. We climbed down towards it. Nothing was left of the prow but a splintered stump. The planking had been broken away by the remorseless beating of the waves, though now the shingle had built up around it, and it stood high and dry. It must have been some years since it came to grief there.

I stood and leaned against one of the upstanding ribs, resting after the scramble across the stones. I felt my blood chill in my veins before the reason for cold dread dawned on my mind. I was reminded so strongly of something . . . surely I had been here before, just here, looking at the bare bones of this ship. . . . No. It was not here. It was on the beach at home. The timbers were bare then because we had not yet made the sides. I knew this ship because I had built her.

Garulf's answer to my question jerked me back to the present.

'I think you should know what this is,' he said.

It was on the tip of my tongue as he said it to ask him if any of the seafarers had survived; he had answered me clearly enough. And now I remembered why the face of the man who sat beside him on the first night we were here had disturbed me – he was one of Gefwulf's crew; one of those who had melted away from our doors into the mists of that dreadful night.

After this I no longer found the days pleasant, for I was afraid of what fate might spring upon us; and I was eager to take the boy and go. But Hnaef was contented to linger.

And now the year was drawing towards autumn. The few trees in Finnsburg were turning golden in the pale sun, and the fires were more and more welcome in the halls at night. The cold closed in early that year, as though to warn us of the fearful winter ahead, and even Hnaef began to think of the journey home. But Finn did not seem ready to see us go, and kept his son close beside him, and we could see how the parting would grieve him. Yet it was cold; and a dark wind from the north broke through the fair weather every few days, making it seem urgent that we should go before winter made land routes impassable and sea routes perilous.

'Wait yet a little,' said Finn. 'Soon many of these my thanes go home, and others come to take their places, and for the few nights when all are here together, we feast and celebrate, and exchange news. Those are the best days of the year in Finnsburg. Stay for them.'

'Till then, but no longer,' agreed Hnaef.

So we made ready to leave, and stayed on. Everyone was restless, and men drifted down to the shore at all hours of the day to look for a sail coming up from the south. The summer thanes were thinking of their families, and of the pleasures of Dorestead, and were ready to go; Hnaef was eager to get his nephew home and begin making a man of him. Finn waited with an aching and divided heart, longing to see again the friends who would come, sorry to part with friends who would go, sorry to lose the companionship and the glory of a visiting king at his court, and both proud and anguished that his son was to leave him. And Hildeburg was torn between the grief of seeing her brother and her son depart, and the joy of seeing Garulf a man under his uncle's protection.

I too was divided; Finn seemed to me still, as he had seemed long ago, the best of men, brave and gracious, and I thought it good to be with him in his halls. But I was haunted by the ghost of a dead ship and a living man.

When I heard we were to wait for the arrival of the new party my misgivings grew deeper, and I spoke to Finn.

'Are there any Jutes among those who come?' I asked him.

'Many. I have never turned away an exile who offered to serve me, no matter whence he came.'

'Then are there any who have not sworn the oath you told us of before we came?'

'None. I took oaths from them all before they left in spring. Have no fear, Hengest. My thanes are all men of honour, and they are deeply sworn.'

At last the ship came. There was a joyful meeting of

old friends, from which we stood aloof, withdrawing to our own hall to let men talk with each other out of the hearing of strangers. Then when the feast began we took our places in the hall. I found myself sitting opposite Gefwulf. He did not like to sit thus with his eyes on a level with mine. We looked away from each other. But when Hnaef came in I saw a flash of hatred on Gefwulf's face, and I knew I was right to fear him.

The feast was splendid and joyful. There was an abundance of new wine from Dorestead, which had come up in the holds of the ships, and men drank deeply, and the talk grew wild. The harp was passed round among us when the fires were already low, and the horns had been filled and filled again. Most of the singers were too drunk to sing, and slurred their words, and cursed themselves, and told bawdy stories instead. And the rest of us were so drunk that we found this funny and roared with laughter at the helpless singers.

Then someone cried out 'Take the harp to the king of the Jutes!' The man whose face I had known and not known got up, and took the harp. He came staggering up the space between the benches, too drunk to walk straight. But when he reached the top of the tables where the noble thanes sat he stopped short of Hnaef's chair, and held out the harp to Gefwulf. Suddenly there was silence. And most of the men there were sober enough to reach for their swords. Then someone belched loudly, and the tense moment passed in loud roars of laughter. I gave the man a push towards Hnaef, and he fell over Hnaef's feet, mumbling, 'King of the Jutes or king of the Half-Danes, which do they mean, how am I to know . . .' and his drunkenness or feigned drunkenness covered the insult.

Hnaef sang a song about the wanderer who longs for

home. All applauded him. And then he leant over, and gave the harp to Gefwulf.

Gefwulf sang. 'Great is the fame of Finnsburg, the fortress of our king. Mighty is his name upon the seas. Over the far sea roads his people go, and when the storm is cold and the winds howl round them, they think of the warm fires in this hall, of the good friends and good food which wait for them here, and they are cheered. Great is the goodness of our prince; his people do not fear to suffer hard sea journeys for his sake, for they know how generously he will reward them. And the doors of this hall are open to all men. Many the poor wanderer, the heart-broken exile who has found a haven here. Never has a man been driven forth comfortless from these doors, to carry wrongs smarting for revenge!'

There were few left sober to hear him. Hnaef was white and Finn was flushed with anger, but nothing was said, lest words should be tinder to straw. Gefwulf put down the harp, and as he did so he looked across at me with some message in his eyes, some urgent thing to make me understand. I looked away. I counted up our numbers, and glancing rapidly round I counted the number of Gefwulf's Jutes.

'Let us sleep off the wine, now,' said Finn, rising.

I went round the tables, shaking and waking sleepy men, and making sure that they all went back to our hall, before I went out into the night myself.

Chapter Seven

My head swam, and the torches which lit our staggering way across to our own hall, spun and whirled and lurched in the hands of the servants. We did not go to our own beds but collapsed laughing and sprawling on the floor, shouting insults at each other, and many of us fell asleep where we lay. But I grabbed at one of the pillars of oak which held up the roof, and stood propped against it, trying to remember why I had decided not to sleep that night. At last my head cleared, and I remembered and went outside.

The cold air sobered me up. Finnsburg was quiet, bathed in the steady icy light of her northern moon. No torches, no fires to make warm sparks, no voices or footfalls to break the faint whisper of the distant sea. I stepped back into the shadows of the doorway, where I could not be seen, and waited.

The air seemed still, and yet the sky was full of movement. Small clouds raced across it, casting rapid patches of darkness on the silent ground. In one of the dark spells I jumped to find Hnaef beside me.

'What do you here out of your bed, my thane?' he asked in a low voice.

'I thought it would be as well to keep a watch tonight, Sire.'

'And so thought I. I have come to watch myself, and I find the door already held. Why do you watch tonight?'

'I have no reason; but I feel danger. Doubtless all

will be well; then no harm will have been done by watching.'

'Wake me when the night is half gone, and I will take a turn,' said Hnaef, and he went back into the darkness of the hall.

I cannot tell you how long I gazed at the black outline of Finn's hall, and the changing moonlight on the unchanging scene. My eyelids drooped, and my head sank forward on my chest, and jerked up again as I drowsed and woke.

And then between the shadowy outlines of the stables on my right, I thought I saw a little flash of light, which disappeared instantly. I was awake at once, the hair pricking on my scalp, my eyes straining into the darkness round the stables. There was nothing to be seen. I looked for a long time, and then at last relaxed my taut limbs, and let my eyes wander over the scene. The moon slid out from behind a cloud, and in her sudden brightness, I saw a sparkling band of points of steely light, moving, flashing, between the great hall and the stables. It was the glint of many spears silvered in the moon.

'Hnaef!' I cried. He was beside me in a moment. Now we could see the bright glinting lights moving towards us from every side, filling the spaces between the buildings with stars of pointed light. And we could hear the dull footfalls of many men treading lightly and moving stealthily.

Hnaef looked. Then he stood in the centre of the hall, and banging his shield with his spear to wake the sleeping men he raised the great battle cry of our people.

'This is no dawn in the east,' he said, his voice rising with excitement, 'nor is it a dragon's flight, nor is it a fire in the gables of the hall, but spears are brought against us!' His voice rang through the hall, and the sleeping heads of his companions were raised from the floor, and the rustling noise of their stirring went through the hall like wind.

'Now woeful deeds will be done,' cried Hnaef, 'bringing harm upon this people! The bird of prey shall sing, the grey wolf howl, the spear shall hiss, and the shield ring against the shaft! So all my thanes awake! Put on your shields, think of your honour, get ready for battle, and be of good courage!'

Even while Hnaef still spoke the torches were lit, and their flickering light showed many fingers where to fasten the buckles and straps of armour. Hnaef's sixty men arose, still in the fine clothes and gold brooches they had worn for the feast, and stood ready, their swords at their sides. Sigeferth leapt to one door with his thane Eaha; at the other door stood Guthlaf and Oslaf, and I myself.

The noise of our awakening reached our enemies, and they ceased trying to take us by surprise, and came onwards in a great rush, and stood in close ranks all round the hall. There was scarcely a face among them we did not know – they were Gefwulf's Jutes, come to break their deep-sworn oaths of peace, and quench the bitter thirst of their hatred in our blood.

'Who would have thought Finn could do this?' said Hnaef behind me, as I stood shoulder to shoulder with Guthlaf in the main door.

'It is not he,' I replied. 'Let no man strike a man of Frisian blood, and Finn will not join in. We will be able to deal with Gefwulf's rabble!'

'Be it Finn's doing or no, strike down all who come against us!' cried Hnaef.

Then the men outside rushed at us, and the fight began. But as I stood locked and swaying in a fatal grip with a man who had taught me to make arrows when I was a boy, I heard at the other door a young voice raised, speaking with a Frisian turn of phrase.

'Who holds the door? Who holds the door?' the light voice cried. 'Against Hnaef only I will not fight. Who holds the door I say?'

'Sigeferth is my name,' came the reply. 'I am a famous wanderer, hardened in many battles, tempered by many sorrows. Fate gives either death or victory now to you and me!'

And with that the din of battle rang from the other door also.

The fight was fierce and brief. We were heavily outnumbered, and completely surrounded, but it took only three men in line, their shields locked together, to hold each door, and there was room for only three of the attackers to face and fight them at a time. Man for man we were more than a match for them, for there are no fighters in the world like the Danes, and we had been in battle more recently than most of the foe. We struck them down as fast as they could come at us, and soon the piles of dead and wounded men at our feet, lying one on top of another where they fell, tripped and hampered the attackers.

Above the loud din of the fighting about our ears we could dimly hear uproar in Finnsburg; cries and running feet filling the town, and torches carried hither and thither at a run. A pale dawn was breaking, and at last Gefwulf's men broke and scurried away from us, leaving us panting and unharmed in our doorways. We had the advantage, for they had given only a few shallow wounds in return for the heaped bodies they had left.

Hnaef stood in the middle of the hall, and asked if there were any of his good men dead. Then he gave orders for the bodies to be cleared from the doors. The dead we dragged out a little way, and left them lying in the dust, the wounded we carried half-way across the yard between the two halls, and left them for their friends to rescue. And as we worked we heard the dull hum of many voices, and of comings and goings in the town, but near us there was a great silence.

'We are in a desperate plight,' said Hnaef, 'if Finn takes vengeance for these thanes of his we have killed.'

'He will not hold us to blame, since they broke faith, and we could do nothing but defend ourselves,' I said, sure of my words; but even as I spoke the last few bodies were uncovered at our feet, and there lay Garulf.

He wore no armour, being still too much a boy to have any, and he had been killed by the first blow of Sigeferth's spear, which pierced his leather jerkin and slid through his ribs to his heart. The yellow cloak he wore was dark with the blood of his companions, who had fallen on top of him, but the sword Hnaef had given him was clasped in his hand with the unsheathed blade still bright and clean, and innocent of blood. His childish face was calm, with the bright colour still on the cheeks, as though he had fallen asleep, and but a touch would wake him. But he did not stir as we carried him gently into the hall, and laid him down at Hnaef's feet. Nobody spoke a word, and the dread of words was on every face. We stood and looked at the murdered boy, the son of our host, the sister's son of our lord Hnaef, and there was not one among us who would not have given his own life gladly if it could have brought back life to that slight form. Hnaef stood staring with wide eyes, and said nothing.

In the end it was Guthlaf who spoke, and he said no word of pity for the child.

'This will be death to us all,' he said.

'Ah, my nephew, my sister's son!' cried Hnaef. 'What

evil adviser, what ill spirit brought you to fight against me? You have destroyed your family, and your blood will cost the spilling of more blood and more again before you are forgotten in death. Now I am steeped in dishonour, stained with the blood of my own kin, and how shall I justify what we have done to you, and how to hold up my head and look Finn in the face?' With that he knelt down, and took the boy's head on his lap, and bowing his own head he wept silently, so that we turned away.

'This is woman's talk!' cried Oslaf. 'Shall we not fight with those who attack us as we sleep? Shall we not fight those who kill their guests?'

Then the guards at the door said, 'Look who comes here!' We crowded the doors to see. Finn came. He wore black, and walked among his oldest and most trusted thanes. And before him came two servants dragging a body by the heels. Its hands were bound behind its back, and round its neck was the rope it had been hanged in. They brought it near enough for us to see that it was Gefwulf, and then they let it lie. And they stood and looked towards us, but they said nothing. Finn had avenged the broken oath. Anger and pride, and shame were marked upon Finn's face, so that I wanted to cry out to Hnaef, 'It was not he! Gefwulf betrayed him, he did not want this harm!' But Hnaef would not come to the door to look and at last Finn and his people turned away, and guards were set at a distance round the hall.

Something was happening in the town. We saw many horses taken from the stables and ridden hard away, and there were men running everywhere, as though searching for something.

And then at about noon Hildeburg came out and stood before the doors, alone, and called to Hnaef. He left Garulf and went to the door.

'My brother,' she said softly, 'I cannot find Garulf. Did he fight at your side last night, and is he with you now?'

Hnaef groaned aloud at the pain of her question.

'He fought last night, sister. Would that it had been at my side! And he is with us. I will bring him to you!'

He signed to me, and I took up the boy in my arms, and carried him out towards her. But when she saw him come she threw up her eyes to the unfeeling sky, and cried the long terrible scream of grief for the dead, and her wailing voice echoed and re-echoed between the halls, and the Frisians came silently up from all sides, so that I put him down hurriedly, and ran back to the shelter of the hall. The wail of grief was taken up by many voices far and near, and we could hear the keening and moaning in the other hall for many hours after they had taken Garulf away.

With this ceaseless dirge in our ears we laboured. We put all the food and ale which stood ready for our journey home in the middle of the hall to be carefully shared out. We climbed into the roof timbers and tore holes in the thatch to give lookout places, and perches whence we could throw down spears; we hacked slits in the wooden walls to make places for spearmen, and we built barricades round the doors so that a dozen men at a time could stand outside and fight. To make these barricades we stripped the hall of all the wood we could move, even cutting away some of the roof supports.

And at evening, when the blood-red sun stood just on the brink of the horizon, Finn came against us. From all parts of the town his men came carrying spears and naked swords, streaming up the roads towards us, their weapons flashing in the scarlet light, blazing where Gefwulf's had glinted cold, so that it looked as though all Finnsburg were on fire.

I remember through a haze of time how hard we fought. We fought as desperate men, for our defeat was death, and like cornered wolves we had nowhere to run to. Finn, I think, fought with a bleeding heart, and no stomach for the work. I know we cut his men down by the dozens as they came against us, hacking at them from behind our barricades, striking them down with flying spears as they crossed the yard towards us.

After two days of this Finn's men came only in sudden runs with long hours of quiet in between. We were even able to recover our spears, dragging them from the bodies of the slain, and running back to cover with no man to stop us. But we grew tired. We had lost not a single man, but all of us had slight wounds, and slowly our strength was lessening. And Finn kept coming. His losses were terrible, but he still fought. We had lost all count of how many Frisians we had killed, but we wondered how long Finn would go on sending them to die upon our blades.

Hnaef's Danes were indeed good fighters. In all my long life I have never seen courage like theirs. They were ill men to live with, with their dark ways, and their sour tongues, but they were good men to have at one's side when it came to a fight.

And Hnaef himself was a Dane in this. He fought like the bear of the great forest, and the bright gleam of Hunlafing in his hand flashed from the heart of the fiercest scuffles. He had never seemed so much a king to me as now, urging us on, keeping up our spirits, and shouting defiance of our enemies, in the face of certain defeat.

And what of Garulf now? Did we remember him? What of Finn? Did we remember that we were his guests? It would have been death to remember it. But the name that we cursed was that of Gefwulf, who had set loose the hateful strokes of battle upon us and upon Finn alike.

It was on the morning of the fifth day that the last attack came. We were tired and worn with thirst, for our packs had not contained water, and we had run out of wine. In the break of dawn we saw them coming out to meet us. And this time Finn came himself. He wore golden armour, and upon his Roman helm there fluttered a plume of purple. And he brought with him the last and best of his thanes. All those who had sat highest at his tables, all those whose names we had heard upon his lips, summer and winter thanes, the flower of Finnsburg, walked at his side as he came. When I saw which door he came to I went to the other one. How could I fight him wearing the ring-shirt he had given me? But at that other door I fought savagely enough. Soon there were three men who had tasted death at my hands. The fighting was bitter indeed; as though we had been playing before and were now in earnest. And this time the men who fell back into the hall were not nursing mere scratches; the dead and dying lay on the foul rushes, and the groans of our own friends tormented our ears. Twenty of our brave sixty fell in a single hour; but at least as many of the Frisians also fell.

'Fight on!' I cried above the tumult. 'There will be no end to this while a single man is alive in Finnsburg to swing a sword!'

But as I spoke there came a great cry from the other door. Reeling back from the blows of the Frisians, his sword hanging slack, his helmet split, and the dark blood streaming from it a warrior came staggering and fell. It was Hnaef. A shout of dismay arose from among us.

'My lord! Hnaef, Hnaef has fallen!' And as soon as those outside heard it they melted away, drifting from the doors and disappearing among the halls of Finnsburg like leaves in the wind, and we were left alone.

We laid Hnaef down beside the cold hearth, and eased the helmet off his head. I remember still how my heart leapt to see that it was only a shallow gash in his head, one not beyond hope. But in the same moment I saw that a scarlet patch was spreading silently across his ring-shirt below the ribs, and blood was trickling down over the linked mail. There was no movement from Hnaef for a long time, and then he opened his eyes and lay staring for many minutes. Guthlaf bent over him, and put a cup drawn from the dregs of the wine to his lips. Slowly Hnaef rolled his staring eyes round the circle of men standing over him, and his mouth shaped our names one by one, but no sound escaped him. Now there were bowed heads and stinging eyes among us, and we knelt round him, waiting for the ghosts of words from his silent lips. As we watched he slowly ran his tongue over his dry lips, once and then again. Then at last he managed to speak, and his words were so unexpected I thought he was raving.

'Mead . . . mead . . .' he said.

'Alas, Sire,' said Oslaf with a groan, 'we are besieged, and there is nothing we can give you to drink.'

'I will bring the blood of Finn to quench your thirst!' cried Guthlaf. But Hnaef struggled on with what he was saying.

'For all . . . all the sweet mead you have drunk in my hall,' he said slowly, 'I am well paid. Never did thanes better repay their lord.'

And then indeed we wept. I remember the salt taste of those desolate tears, and how long we stayed motionless round Hnaef's unmoving body, till I thought he was dead. But his eyelids fluttered and lifted once more, and he said softly,

'Hengest, where is Hengest?' He tried to raise his

head, and Guthlaf and Oslaf beside him lifted him into a sitting position.

'I am here,' I said standing before him.

'Take . . .' he said with a feeble movement of his hand, 'take Hunlafing!'

So I stooped over him, and took the sword again, and as I did so I suddenly saw the sulky youth whom I stooped over in the halls of Sigehere long ago, when I laid Hunlafing in his lap. It was I who gave it, and it was I who took it again. It was from Finn I had it long ago, and it was for Finn I took it now, and the burden of vengeance which went with it fell on me.

Hnaef seemed not to have finished speaking, and his eyes were still open, and fixed on me, but his head rolled back, and then he had finished with all words for ever.

I took the sword, and went into a dark corner, and sat and brooded over my grief and my helplessness. I was now the lord and leader of Hnaef's men; the loneliness of the leader swept over me, and I could not see how to lead or defend these men. In the morning Finn would come again, and all would be over. With our weary bodies, our shattered weapons, our numbers all but halved, and our hearts sick with grief we could not stand against him even for an hour. I even cursed him for the sense of honour which made him fight rather than set fire to the hall. At least we could all have perished together in the flames. So the night dragged on towards dawn. The voices and movements in the hall died away, and when at last the grey light of morning crept between the shattered doorposts the living slept beside the dead, and I was the only man there awake.

And so when I heard Finn's voice calling me from outside I went out to meet him alone.

Finn too was alone. He stood unarmed in the middle of

the yard between the halls. His face was haggard and pale, and his arm was bound up in white linen, and supported in a sling. For a long moment we stared at one another.

'I have come to make a truce with you, Hengest,' he said. Black anger seared me.

'Shall I make a treaty with the killer of my lord?' I cried. 'I shall die in your blood-stained guest hall sooner than talk with you!'

'Which think you is the harder, my friend,' said Finn softly in reply, 'to make terms with the killers of one's lord, or to make terms with the killers of one's son?'

At that I had no anger left to pit against him.

'Why do you offer this?' I asked.

'Most of my thanes lie dead,' said Finn. 'I cannot fight it out with you to a finish.' I said nothing. We had killed more men than I could keep count of, yet I could scarcely believe him.

'Come and see,' said Finn.

I walked beside him across to the great hall, and stood in the doorway. The hall was full of the stench of blood and death, and great numbers of men lay dead and dying upon the rushes. The wounded sat upon benches and leant against the walls, and the handful of unhurt men sat round the fire, their heads drooping with weariness, and misery.

It certainly did not look as if Finn could win any battle with these men. Yet it did not seem to me that mine could fight more either.

'Come you and see,' I said to him. So we retraced our steps and looked in from the doorway at the same pitiful scene of pain and death and weariness. Finn turned his face to mine, and his eyes pleaded with me though his head was held high.

'A man must accept what is decreed by the fates, however bitter it may be. We must make a treaty, you and I, because we can do nothing else. Surely it was not in your heart, or in mine that this battle was made. And you know that I wished it not, and I know that you wished it not. We need not hate each other unto death, since we are both guiltless of this blood.'

'What else can we do?' I mused. 'We cannot even die if we cannot fight. We will make a treaty with you, Finn.'

I thought I might have trouble getting my men to accept it, but the flame of anger had been quenched by weariness and the sickness that comes upon men after great slaughter. Great wrong had been both given and received, and neither we nor Finn had started it.

And so we laid down our swords, and swore a great oath with Finn, and the battle ended.

Chapter Eight

These were the terms of the treaty we made with Finn. We agreed that all the survivors should share the great hall; and that the Frisians should clear a whole row of benches and a high seat for my party. We would serve Finn, and when he gave gifts to the men who sat in his hall we should receive rings and old treasures, and plated gold just as often as the Frisians. And we swore that nobody should break the truce in word or deed; that no biting words should rebuke us for following the slayer of our own ring-giving lord, since we were forced to it. If any man spoke words which brought the battle to mind, then the sword's edge should silence him. No man of any nation should carry weapons in the hall. And with the agreement of his council Finn swore to hold us in honour. If Finn himself had started the attack on us we would all have died rather than compound with him; but the harm done and the harm taken between us were equally grievous, and we both had more cause to blame Gefwulf, whom Finn had killed, than to blame each other.

We swore deeply on our gods, and on our honour.

And then the burning of the dead began. We worked for two days building two great pyres, twenty and more feet across, and longer than they were wide. We had to cut peat from the marshes and drag it back to Finnsburg, and we tore down the broken hall, and used the wood from that. When at last the fires were ready we brought out the dead. We laid them side by side, their broken weapons in their cold hands, their shattered shields upon them. Finn brought up from his gold-hoard the sacred gold to give as gifts to the dead, and many a ring and goblet was laid among the slain. It was a cool day, with a clear blue sky, high and still, and the sound of the sea louder than usual in our ears. We ran to and fro, carrying bodies, and trappings, clambering up and down the huge piles of tinder, all busy with the work. Many were the blood-stained corselets, the helms adorned with golden swine, the boars' heads made of hard iron which we laid out there. Many and noble were the dead!

At last we brought out Hnaef himself, and laid him in the midst of the scattered gold, in the centre of the pyre with his men around him. At his feet we poured out the mead he loved, and at his head we laid his banner. Then we had done, and a hush fell upon us and we stood silent, waiting.

At the other end of the yard the Frisians too had finished loading their dead on to the fires, and they too stood still, with the silent awe of the ceremony creeping over them. And as we stood thus Hildeburg came out of the women's chamber and behind her came six women bearing Garulf on a stretcher. She had wrapped him in a purple cloak, and his unhelmeted head was bound with a fillet of gold. Slowly, with all eyes upon them, they advanced towards the Frisian pyre. But they did not stop there. They came on towards us.

'Lay him at his uncle's side!' said Hildeburg in a clear voice. While we stood watching, Garulf was lifted up, and laid beside Hnaef, and the strands of his bright hair blew in the light wind across the dark iron ring-mail on Hnaef's shoulder. And so they went on their journey together as they should have gone.

Then we put flames to the dry wood and stood back.

Round and round both fires went Hildeburg and her women, stepping slow, and singing, a grief-laden lament. Their voices were solemn at first, and then rose to a wild and heart-rending wailing as the flames mounted. It took a long time for the fires to burn. We stood watching for many minutes while the licking flames crept upwards. And then a wind came off the sea, and fanned them, and from the laden timber a roaring sound came which grew so loud that the voices of the mourners were drowned in it, and the bright fire leapt up between the bodies on top of the piles, and licked hungrily round them. A column of smoke rose high into the cloudless sky, and the fearless spirit of Hnaef went with it. In the fierce heat of the flames the helmets melted on the heads of the slain. The greedy fire devoured all of both peoples who had fallen in battle. And now their glory was gone.

When we could no longer see even the outlines of the

bodies of our friends, we went silently from the fires, and sat around in low-voiced and gloomy mood in the cool of the great hall. It was three days and three nights before the fires died down to smouldering ashes, and three days after that, even though a light rain began to fall, before the ashes were cold. All those days Hildeburg did not leave her watch over them but sat silently beside the Jutish pyre, or walked round in the circle of the mourner. Finn came often and sat with her in the dust. Guthlaf and Oslaf and I myself were the other most patient watchers over the dying fires.

As soon as the ashes were cold, and the time of grief was over, Finn's men started to busy themselves making ready their long-delayed ship. For many of the survivors were men who had been all summer at Finnsburg, and now were due to go home. There were so few men left that there was difficulty in finding men to crew the ship to take them; but at last they were ready. Finn wept when he said farewell to them, and they were weighed down with grief at the thought of the dear lost friends who should have sailed with them. But off they went at last, to their homes and their high city of Dorestead, and none too soon for the storms of winter were upon us.

When they were gone a great calm fell. There were empty places at the tables and broken circles round the fires, and the places were filled by aching memories of the men who were gone. Ghosts lurked in the shadows, and many men went about with grief for the loss of friend or kinsman crushing their hearts, and angry words sticking in their throats. None dared to joke, or drink deeply, but we lived in gloom and fear.

When the ship had been gone about a week, Guthlaf and Oslaf found me alone, as I stood tending my horse in the stables. They stood side by side, their faces dark and stony, as they had been ever since Hnaef's death.

'What do you mean to do?' asked Guthlaf.

'And when will it be done?' said Oslaf. I gazed at them in a long silence. It had not occurred to them that I might keep my oath to Finn; they thought only of how and when it should be broken, and more blood be spilt to quiet the blood already shed.

'It is a hard matter to know what should be done,' I said. They were silent a little. Guthlaf regarded me with doubt and hatred in his eyes.

'It seems a clear enough thing to me,' he said at last.

'The man who started the fight is already dead,' I said.

'But not the slayer of Hnaef. He walks in the warm sun and eats and drinks, and feels not the heat of the funeral fire, nor the clammy cold of the silent earth.'

'Who is to know what hand struck down Hnaef?'

'We all know that it was the hand of a man sworn in the service of Finn!'

'So now are we all.'

'Do you mean then, to keep this oath?' asked Guthlaf, his voice laden with biting scorn.

'I think it is an oath which cannot be kept,' I answered slowly. 'But I look to see it broken from Finn's side first.' They shook their heads angrily.

'Do you not see,' I continued, 'that it is on Finn that this truce weighs most heavily? He has lost a son, the heir to his princedom, and to all Frisia; and more he has lost the flower of his men, of his dear friends, for each of whom he would have taken vengeance in blood against any other killer. And it is from his treasury that our rewards must come. Do you think he can keep his hatred and sorrow unspoken for ever? And as soon as he utters a word against us, or offers us the smallest slight he has broken his word. Finn's is indeed an oath which cannot be kept. But I will keep this truce until he breaks it, for it seems to me that the terms were fair, and I would rather avenge Hnaef honourably than dishonourably.'

'In that case, we ask you to let us go. We are men of Sigehere's first, and took service with Hnaef on his orders. Now Hnaef is dead we will return to him. Let us go.'

'How will you go now, with the storms of winter on the seas, and the land flooded and perilous?'

'Give us a ship and we will go.'

'It is a wild thing to make a journey on the seaways now,' I said.

'Better to take that chance, better to drown!' cried Guthlaf, 'than to spend the winter as you mean to spend it, fawning upon a murderer!'

My hand flew to my sword hilt, but I held back my anger.

'In what you say I shall see your great love of Hnaef, and not the insult,' I replied.

'Let us go,' said Oslaf coldly.

And so I went to Finn and asked him for a ship to send them on their way. And when they were gone, there seemed to be suddenly fewer grim faces around the hall. We breathed easier, and a little laughter and comradeship began slowly to grow among us.

And we needed it. For the great winds from the north blew upon Finnsburg now, and the wild snow came on the winds from over the sea. The snow fell deep for week upon week, and the wind blew it into great drifts around the town, and life became hard. We had to dig in the frozen snow for peat for our fires, and fowling became difficult and unprofitable. The cold wind blew through the hall, freezing us as we sat clustered round the best

fires we could make, and we had to thaw the wine and mead in the great pitchers before we could drink the welcome blood-warming draughts. I forget how long the snow went on. I remember how with our shrunken numbers we were hard put to it to find food and fuel, and how we lived cooped up together in the hall, grumbling at our discomfort, and drawn together in grudging friendship and cheer by sheer need. Finn poured out strong drink freely to keep us warm, and although we were all packed so close there were no quarrels at first.

Each day we struggled through the snow-filled streets to do our share of the work of the town; watching on the walls, though what enemy could have come upon us in that weather I do not know, or searching for firewood, or fowling, or helping the common folk to drag the nets up the beaches, for no ships could put out to fish in the bay, and in the sharp necessity in which we stood all differences of rank were forgotten, and thane helped churl to win fish from the furious waves. It was dreadful work for the wind lashed even the water in the sheltered bay into great waves which knocked men over, and sucked them under if they lost their footing in the savage pull of the backswirl. The fishes brought out of this raging water in the nets thrown from the beach were small and few, but they were greatly needed.

Then at last the storm blew itself out, and the wind dropped. For the first time in many days the paths we cleared through the snow were not filled with deep drifts again the next day; and so we could walk around the town and stretch our legs, and visit the more distant houses.

On the third day of the calm I went to walk along the wall and look at the great white plains which glittered unendingly as far as the eye could see, broken only by a few dark patches of water on the marsh. As I walked, holding my cloak close around me, for the cold was sharp, I met a party of women walking in the other direction. One of them wore a mantle of richly embroidered stuff, but even so it was not at the first glance that I recognized Hildeburg. She had not come to the hall to sit among us since the fight. She had changed. Her face was no longer beautiful. She was thin and the bones of her face were gaunt, and cast dark shadows under the cheekbones. Her lovely eyes were pale and lustreless, and rimmed with red, spoiled by much weeping. And her hair was lightly streaked with the colourless grey of old age. This too, I thought, shocked at what I saw, is another harm to Finn which we have done.

'I was hoping to see you, Hengest,' she said, and I was startled to hear her familiar voice unchanged from so changed a face.

'Walk with me.'

I turned and walked beside her, and for a while we said nothing.

'This is indeed a hard place to winter in,' I said, 'I am not surprised that Finn does not ask his men to stay here two winters running. Do you not wish to be safe and warm in Dorestead?'

'No,' she said simply, 'I had rather be with Finn.'

'Once, long ago, we spoke of him before,' I said. 'Do you remember?' She nodded. 'And what I said of him then was true?'

'Most true,' she said. 'You are an old friend, Hengest, and more than a friend, perhaps. I am wrong to be afraid to speak to you. And yet I am afraid of everything now.'

'You have suffered greatly,' I said.

'Yet it is not the loss that I have suffered, terrible though it is to lose a brother and a son in a single day, which weighs upon my heart most cruelly,' she said softly. 'It is the fear of what may be yet to come. Tell me, Hengest, tell me truly what is in your heart. Are your thoughts grim?'

'Lady, I have lost the lord I followed, and with him many friends. When I think of this my thoughts are indeed grim.'

She hesitated. Then she said, 'Ah, Hengest, do you mean us any harm?'

'The gods blast me,' I cried, 'if I have ever wished any harm on you!'

'But when you think of Finn what do you think? Do you hate him?'

'Hate Finn! No!' I exclaimed. Still she had not done with me. 'But do you think ill of him and judge him harshly in your heart?'

'No, Lady,' I said gravely. 'I wish indeed that I were

such a man as he is.' And then she was satisfied, as she had been long ago, and we talked of other things till we came to the door of her house, and there I left her.

That night I watched Finn more closely than usual. He sat among us, talking of the snow, and then of Dorestead, and then of the trade on the northern route, and the price of furs. He listened to the song of the minstrel, he joked, and laughed at the coarse joking of Eaha the Dane. He looked on all of us, of either party with equal friendliness; I could not catch the slightest frown cast on any of us; but when for a moment he was not talking or listening, his face fell into an expression of sadness as naturally as it had once expressed boyish eagerness. Finn too had changed. I was glad I had no glass in which to look at my own face, for fear of what I might see there.

When I woke the next day, and went out of doors there was a difference in the air. The cold cut to the bone, and all the water was frozen hard. Several pitchers of wine had cracked open in the night, and the thawing snow hung frozen in long icicles fringing the gables, the cleared paths were glazed with ice on which I could scarcely stand; yet it was none of this which seemed so strange. I struggled to name what the change was. Then at last I realized; the sound of the sea had gone. Impossible! I strained my ears, and then I heard it, but very far and faint. I ran down to the walls to look.

There was no sea between the shore and the long spit of shingle; there was a stretch of ice! The sea itself had frozen. And beyond the shingle bar, in the wide ocean I could see lumps of ice, floating, tossed to and fro on the muffled waves. The men of Finnsburg gathered to look and exclaim. Nobody could remember such a thing happening before. Some of the Danes had seen it in the northern seas around Norway; but no one had heard of it so far south. We shivered and wondered how we would do without fish.

About that at least we need not have worried. The fish were easier to catch now. The fishermen made holes in the ice, which was thick enough to walk on, and put bait in the nets trailed through the holes. We could walk right across the harbour, out to the shingle, and it felt strange indeed to know that there was deep water under one's feet.

Finn said that it was a great wonder, and he opened his treasury, and gave out gifts for us to remember it by. We scanned the gifts closely enough, but we could not discover that he had given more generously to his own men than to us. And they looked carefully too, and could not find themselves disadvantaged.

The supply of fish was better, but so slowly that one scarcely noticed how it happened everything else grew worse. The cold was cruel, and we suffered badly from it. Draughts in the hall were like daggers piercing us through, and men quarrelled as they tried to move their beds out of the draughts, and took each other's places. It was so dreadful to go out, even by day, that we stayed round the fire in the hall all we could, and we were cramped and cross. All day we were packed close together, and we began to hate each other. The thick accents of the Danes, the light accents of the Frisians got on our nerves, and sounded like the grunts of pigs, or the stupid sing-song of idiots. Exasperated, we would go outside to get away from each other, only to be driven in again almost at once by the cold. And this got worse from day to day.

Often Finn had to settle quarrels, and sometimes they came to blows. And although I watched him like a hawk, waiting for the slightest movement of its prey, I could not find that he was harder on one side than the other when he punished men who quarrelled. Though it was indeed hard to the point of impossibility, Finn kept his oath to us.

And I knew how hard it was. I knew how the choking anger battered his heart, and what strength of soul he needed to keep its scalding upsurge locked within him, and keep his face still and calm; I knew how the empty place beside him where Garulf would have sat haunted him, emptying all things of joy for him. I knew how our faces in place of those other well-loved faces were hateful to him, and I knew how the friendship there had been between him and me when we were boys tormented him now. I guessed that Hildeburg had questioned him too, and that he had said, 'Hate Hengest? No!'

I knew and guessed these things because I felt them for myself. I too was holding back my hand from vengeance. I hated the living for the sake of the dead. I never sat down first among my men, or took the first sip from the brimming drinking-horn without feeling the sharp absence of the lord who should have sat and drunk before me. Wherever I went the ghost of Hnaef walked with me. I shivered in the inhospitable cold; but I thought that it was warmer where I stood than in the dark earth where Hnaef's ashes lay scattered. And I wore a different sword now. It hung at an odd angle from my belt, for the buckle did not fit well. And it was heavier, with all its jewels, than the plain one I was used to. At every step I took the ring on the hilt clinked against the linked mail of my shirt. They rang together in protest when I walked up the hall to take my gifts from Finn's hands; the extra weight of it seemed to slow my steps as I went about my duties in Finn's town. I was driven night and day by my restless heart; I well knew what Finn suffered and what it cost him to keep faith with us. And the longer I watched him the greater his courage and truth seemed to me, and the more deeply I loved him, and with every day which passed, the vengeance I owed to Hnaef seemed more terrible to me.

I think Finn feared as I did, that with each day of the cold, as men's tempers frayed, the danger to us all grew greater. The peace was not kept for long; one night a Frisian, enraged at some small offence, cried out against Sigeferth as a traitor, a perfidious guest and false to his lord. The wild words woke echoes in every man who heard them, and had we not all been drowsy I think we would have slaughtered each other then and there, but before any other man could act Finn sprang down from his place, and struck the accuser dead at our feet. Then he turned away and went slowly out of the hall. I followed him, but when I saw the look on his face as he cleaned his sword, I turned away and left him to master his grief alone. Finn had lost another of his men; but we were saved from disaster. I warned my own men sternly that I would deal likewise with any foolish tongues among them.

Thus the long winter dragged on, and thus we lived, dealing graciously with each other like brothers, lest we should butcher each other like cattle. And all through the long nights I tossed in my cold bed, kept wakeful by my divided heart. Sometimes I thought of Finn; how good he was and how true, how he had lost his son and his thanes, and yet been fair and gracious. But he had taken revenge for Garulf first. And then I thought of Hnaef, who was dead, who had been treacherously set upon when he was an unoffending guest in another man's house – Hnaef struck down in his youth with glory yet to win, and all those brave men with him, who had fought so well and stoutly against hopeless odds. And I remembered how he had found Garulf dead, and mourned him, so that his last few hours had been darkened with sorrow, and then I thought of Gefwulf whose revenge this had been – Gefwulf who set nephew against uncle, who sat and ate with us at table while he planned his treason, who had unsheathed the sword, and set it thirsting for the blood which once tasted it must drink and drink again ere its desire be slaked. Surely Gefwulf was a wicked man, and Finn did ill to shelter him, and receive him as a thane.

But yet . . . Gefwulf too had been wronged. I remembered how he had come home to be insulted, to find himself stripped of wealth and honour, and all given to a stranger from an enemy land; how he had been felled in the dust, and how Hnaef who should have shielded him had laughed. Had not Hnaef brought troubles upon his own head? And yet he was a guest in another man's house . . . so the thoughts drove round in circles, and my heart was torn between them.

No matter how well I thought of Finn, I could not quiet the ghost of Hnaef, or forget the picture of his pale face uplifted to mine, and his dying lips framing my name, as he gave me his sword, this sword, always at my side; the sword with which I should avenge him; the sword which long ago I had taken from Finn, and carried into Denmark as a gift. How I wished now that Hnaef had broken it, and flung it into the lake of the goddess, as he had nearly done!

But with each step I took in Finnsburg it swung awkwardly at my side.

Chapter Nine

Nothing lasts for ever, nothing good or ill is not carried away by the remorseless flow of time. One morning we were awakened by a strange noise, a creaking, groaning sound. The sentries had seen nothing, and we could find no reason for the sound, but the air was warmer, and the wind was blowing from the sea instead of from the cold north. All day it blew warm, and the sun shone weakly, and the snow began to look wet, with a thin filmy thaw starting upon it. And then in the evening while we sat eating the great noise started. It sounded like the loudest thunder, but it did not come from the sky but from the sea.

Out we all ran, and climbed on to the walls of Finnsburg, while the incredible din crashed round us, creaking, cracking, booming. In the bright light of a full moon we could see the whole shiny expanse of the bay heaving, thrusting great slivers upwards and falling back again, opening in fretted cracks of dark, and roaring and crashing as it moved. The ice was breaking up, and the imprisoned sea was shaking off its fetters. In the morning the sound of the waves rang sharp and clear, as they rolled on to the near-by shore, reminding us painfully by their forgotten familiar sound of the summer before when all things were different. The fragments of ice floated round the bay, knocking together, and washing up on the beach. The first fisherman who put out had his boat smashed under him, and narrowly escaped death, but each day the ice

boulders grew smaller and fewer. And on land our tired eyes could rest from the ceaseless glare on a few patches of green spreading while the snow retreated. Just as it does now, the wonderful bright weather had returned with the spring.

And Finnsburg was beautiful. The grass of the meadows round it was the freshest green I have ever seen, and the rich and tender pastures were full of wild flowers of many kinds, and the dunes of sand along the shore were bright with sea-pinks and the floating sea-flowers in strange colours. The sky over that flat land seemed very high and clear, and the light sparkled like clear water. The great sea rolled on to the beaches, and men worked to repair and refit the ships for the first voyages of spring. The hunting was good, and we ate fresh meat, and all around men were busy and cheerful. But I was unquiet still. I thought of Hnaef's lands left all this time without lord or governor; I thought of my own farms, and woods, and I feared to find that the Danes had taken all at last with no man there to stop them. So I went to speak to Finn.

'We have served you all winter, Finn, and now your men will soon come up from Dorestead to take their turn with you, and you will need us no more. We have had no trouble; but it is not good to tempt fate, or to try men's patience too far. It is not wise that we should remain here. When your new men come, let us go.'

'Where will you go, Hengest?' asked Finn.

'Home.'

'Do you think it safe for you?'

'I doubt it, but a man must go somewhere, and I cannot stay here.'

'Why do you say that? Have I not made you welcome? Have I not been a good lord to you all? I think once when you were young you would have stayed with me willingly enough.'

'Do not talk of it!' I cried. 'You are such a host and such a lord as every man would want. Gladly would I have followed you if the fates had willed it long ago; glad would I be to stay if there were not blood between us. But if I stay, then sooner or later that blood will be remembered. And I think you cannot say that it will not be hard on you if I stay here, and you have to keep that oath of yours for ever!'

'I will keep it either way, whether you go or stay,' said Finn quietly. 'Stay till the ship from Dorestead comes.'

To this I agreed. But no sooner had I made the arrangement with Finn than my heart cried out against me. Was I to leave Hnaef's ashes lying in a strange land unavenged? Was I to run like a coward from the thing I had to do? No, I must stay until Finn broke down, and then I must take vengeance. And when I thought of this, I thought again, 'It is time I was gone. Finn is an honourable man, and I am sworn in his service. I will surely harm him if I stay. Let me be gone from here.'

But I left my going too late.

Finn had sentries scanning the horizon for any sight of the ship which would bring his men from Dorestead. One day as we were mounting our horses to go hunting, the sentry ran into the yard crying that there was a sail. Finn's face lit up.

'They come at last?'

'There is indeed a sail, Sire, but it comes from the north.'

'From the north?' Finn's smile was changed at once to a frown of puzzlement. Then he relaxed. 'Perhaps it will pass by. There are many roads for a ship to follow.'

But an hour later, when we rode out to the shore beyond the bay we saw that the ship was putting in to Finnsburg. And she was a warship. Finn turned his horse, and we rode back at once. We rode briskly, but we did not reach home before the newcomers. When we got back the town was full of excitement, the people grouped and talking in the streets, as men do who have seen something untoward.

Finn did not stop to ask, but rode up to his hall. There we dismounted, and entered.

At the tables near the door sat a group of twenty armed men, their helmets on their heads, and weapons in their hands, hardly like men who come in peace. And at the head of them sat Guthlaf and Oslaf.

I felt the cold fear flowing round my heart. Finn gazed at them silently. Then he said,

'Guthlaf and Oslaf, you are welcome in my halls, as it was agreed between us. But I do not let any man of any nation carry weapons in the hall; nor do I know these whom you bring with you. What of them?'

Guthlaf got slowly to his feet. 'These are men of mine. They do as I say. You have no need to treat them differently from me. If I am welcome, they are welcome also. As for weapons, I am used to carrying them with me.'

Finn considered. 'Your men are welcome. But they

shall keep the terms of our oath. They shall not carry weapons in my hall.' With that he turned and left us.

'I thought you were Sigehere's men, and disdained my service,' I said to them. 'What brings you back to me?'

'It is not to you we return,' said Oslaf, 'but to our sworn lord who will never leave these halls.'

'He has no need of thanes now,' I said. 'Nor will he ever again give out the red gold, or the gleaming gems to his followers. There is little to be gained from seeking him.'

The cold faces of the strangers were turned towards me. There was an ominous silence. Then Guthlaf spoke.

'You were waiting for Finn to break his oath. And you have been here all winter, and you have not moved. Do you mean to say he has kept it?'

'He has kept it,' I said.

'You must have a blind eye for slights, a deaf ear for insults if you have not been able to find fault with him!' said Oslaf with a sneer.

'He has kept it,' I repeated.

'Ah, Hnaef,' said Guthlaf. 'You did ill when you gave Hunlafing to this man. He has no heart for vengeance. He does not find life burdensome while you lie unavenged, he lives at ease and serves your slayer! You would have done better to give your sword to me! As for you, Hengest, you would have done well to refuse the sword if you did not mean to use it.'

His words cut me to the heart, and I turned away from him, and fled to find a place where I could be alone.

How swiftly the sun swung round the sky, and sank towards the sea! It seemed to me I had sat thinking for only a few minutes when dusk drifted down, and the time for the meal came. I waited in the gloom, while all the men in Finnsburg walked over to the hall, and the sound of voices and bustle came forth. Then at last I went over to the porch, unbuckled my sword belt, left it with all the others, and went in.

My seat, just below Finn's, stood empty. Guthlaf and Oslaf had taken the top seats of the row, and their men sat with them. Thus all twenty of them were between me and my own men. I walked up to my place and sat down. Finn turned as I came, and suddenly he smiled at me, a smile of open joy long absent from his face. I was astonished, for there was only fear in my own heart.

'Sing!' cried Finn to the minstrel. The feast began. There was plenty of wine that night, and fine dishes on the table. We ate and drank well, and slowly the talk grew, the usual chaffing talk of ships and horses and suchlike. Then Finn called out to his pages, and four of them came in bearing a great box of oak, and set it before him. From the door behind him Hildeburg came dressed in white and gold, pale and stately, and stood beside him.

'Winter is over,' said Finn, 'and all of you, Jutes and Half-Danes, and my own Frisians have served me well. And now Hengest has asked me leave to go, and lead you to new places. Therefore I will once more give out gifts among you, to show my gratitude before you depart.'

This was the first the newly come Danes had heard of my going, and though my back was turned to them, I sensed the tremor that the news sent down their ranks.

Then Finn took from his box gift after gift, and Hildeburg came bearing them down the hall, giving them to one man after another. They were splendid things; ornaments, jewels, drinking-horns, lodestones, torques of beaten and twisted gold, but not a weapon among them, not so much as a dagger. As always at the giving of gifts the hall was full of exclamations of pleasure, voices thanking

Hildeburg, laughter, and talk as men compared what they had received, each preferring his own. At least all had received something, according to their rank, except Guthlaf and Oslaf and me. Finn gave me another smile. I could see what he was doing. He was showing Guthlaf and Oslaf that he rewarded all alike, as he had sworn to do. He was showing how he kept his oath. He waved to a page, and the boy went outside, and came back leading a pair of grey horses of great beauty. Taking their bridles, Hildeburg led them to Guthlaf and Oslaf. Then she brought to me a splendid falcon on a golden chain. I saw the glint of pleasure in the dark eyes of Guthlaf, but he did not melt his unrelenting silence. And then, when we all thought the giving was over, Finn found from his box a ring of gold for each of the twenty Danes who had newly come, and who had done nothing to earn his bounty. None could say he was not generous to his thanes!

And now the fires burnt lower, and the eating was over, and the wine was sipped instead of swilled from drinking-horns, men grew sleepy, and the drowsy comradeship of the feast spread its mellow warmth among us. Someone started the harp on its way round the tables, and men sang in turn. One or two singers sang comic jingles, and we laughed wildly as men do when they are drunk. Then someone sang a sad song about a drowned man, and at once our mood changed to hazy sadness. One of the Frisians took the harp, and sang a song of grief for lost friends.

'Where are the riders who filled this town with the sound of horses? Where are the fine steeds? Where the plated gold? Where is the laughter which filled these walls, which gladdened the hearts of men in times of old? Where are the arms which raised these walls, the hands which wrought these lovely places? Where are the men of old?'

I think there was no thought among the Frisians or Jutes but that tearful pleasure which comes from listening to a sad tale, but the Danes stiffened in their places, and when the song was over Oslaf stepped forward and took the harp.

Down the hall, over the murmuring voices his harsh alien voice rang out. He struck a loud and mournful chord from the strings, as he sang.

'Dark is the life of a man who must live without a lord. There is no joy for him anywhere on the face of the earth. Alone, and without reward, must he wander in desolate places, and there is no solace for his grief but that of revenge! And thou, Hnaef, what shall I say of thee? Vile was the manner of thy death! Thou wast betrayed, set upon by traitors, killed by thine own host! How my heart groans to think of such wickedness going unavenged!'

His voice was drowned by uproar in the hall. Everyone leapt to his feet, crying out, overturning tables, spilling the wine, shouting and threatening. Men ran for weapons, but the hall doors were closed, and at each there stood a pair of Danes with naked swords in their hands. From under their cloaks the Danes drew swords, and a silence fell as men realized that they were trapped, unarmed.

Oslaf threw away the harp. Leaping on a table he cried out, 'Blood for blood!'

On his high-seat sat Finn, gazing at the chaos below him with horror in his eyes. Already the Danes had fallen upon the helpless Frisians and the cries and screams of the dying rang in our ears.

'Ah, Hnaef,' cried Finn in agony, 'how ill didst thou do to take the Danes for friends. How vile are these thanes of yours!'

Through my mind like the white flash of lightning

there ran the memory of Hnaef saying, 'Never did thanes better repay their lord ...' and with it the memory of how hard and how bravely we had fought against Finn for a life we could not save. And at that instant Guthlaf was at my side, and he thrust Hunlafing into my hands.

That splendid sword was always eager for the thrust, always balanced sweet and tempting in the hand that held it, always hungered for the battle-play. About my ears was the dreadful din of slaughter, my heart was sore from hearing Finn cry out against Hnaef. So I took Hunlafing, and I walked up to Finn, and stood over him in my anger, and struck him. He looked at me with eyes darkened with pain and worse than pain, and then in a fury at his terrible gaze I struck him again and again till he slumped in his chair, and fell in a sea of blood to the floor.

I looked down at him, and then I looked up, and my eyes met those of Hildeburg who stood behind his chair. Then a terrible madness came upon me. I do not remember how many men I killed. I remember nothing.

It was hours later when I came to myself again. The thin grey dawn was just beginning. I was still in the hall, but it took me some time to realize it. I was alone. The floor was covered with smashed dishes, broken tables, torn hangings ripped from the walls, spilt mead and spilt blood, and dead men lying in confusion. It looked as though a tempest had blasted it, leaving only shattered debris behind; and it was quite silent. Not even the sound of a single drawn breath could I hear inside the hall, but outside, in the distance I could hear a noise of shouting, and running and smashing, resounding through Finnsburg. I was dazed, and at first did not realize where I was. Then I knew it, and woe at the destruction overwhelmed me. This hall had been home to us all that

long winter; it was Finn's pride and hope, his own place. I groaned to see it so ruined. Then my eyes, wandering over the chaos, rested on the figure of a man lying face downwards in front of the high-seat. His hair was matted with blood; surely it was that which made it look so red. But he was wearing a purple cloak; the outflung hand glittered; he wore Finn's ring. Then at last my own part in this ruin came back to me, and I remembered what I had done.

I went outside. I ran through the streets of the town. Houses were broken and burning everywhere. A few Frisians cowered in corners, most seemed to have fled. The Danes and Jutes and Half-Danes were masters of the town. They were looting and plundering, staggering under loads of stolen goods, carting all they could lay their hands on to take down to the ships in the harbour. At the top of the main street Guthlaf stood on a barrel to raise himself above the throng, and shouted orders to the hurrying men.

'Find that Jutish woman!' he cried. 'I want her unharmed. She is the last of the royal house, and Sigehere will want her safe.'

'She is here, Guthlaf,' came an answering cry.

'Put her in my ship,' he said. Hildeburg had fainted, I think, for I saw her slumped over the shoulder of a Dane, who carried her off at a run towards the ships. One of her maids ran after her, loyally staying with her mistress.

I stood looking on, still dazed, till Guthlaf turned and saw me.

'Ho, Hengest!' he cried. 'I wondered what had become of you. I have a message for you from Sigehere my king.'

'Well?'

'He says that provided you have the blood of Finn on

your sword you will be welcome and honoured in his court.'

'I will not accept an offer with such a condition joined to it!' I cried angrily.

'Yet your blade is dark; you would do well to accept. Where else will you go? You would be foolish to offend Sigehere, his power stretches far.'

'I will go anywhere on earth so long as it is not with you!' I shouted, and I turned my back on him, and ran down to the shore. There I found a boat; all the ships were already taken, and loaded with plunder. I seized it, and set the first of my men I could find to guard it. The boat would take twelve men, and it had a sail. Then I looked for my dozen men. It was hard work finding them. Most of my party were glad to see the day's work done, and eager to go with the Danes and share the booty in the ships. And it was certain that anyone who came with me would never see his home again. An exile without end, poverty and loneliness were all I had to offer. Yet there were enough to come with me; there were five old men who came because they had served in my father's house, and two young men who came because their fathers were among the five, Wulfhelm, who came because I had saved his life, one who came because he was my cousin, and two who came from the love of wild journeys, and the desire for adventure.

When we had made up the number we spent a frantic hour hastily loading all the food we could find, and all the water jars, and looking for ropes and nails and other things we needed in the devastated stores on the jetties.

I ran past Guthlaf again, as I went in search of grain in the kitchens, and heard him swearing and crying on his gods to blast his men for fools, because in spite of his orders a little party of Frisians had succeeded in reaching the shore, and taking a boat. Their sail was already small on the southern horizon. Never did a ship carry worse news to tell!

As for us, no one tried to stop us. We got away in only two hours, though not quickly enough for me, sickened as I was by the disgusting and brutal scene around me. We hoisted sail and put out to sea, and the last I saw of Finnsburg was the smoking outline of its broken buildings slipping below the horizon behind us.

Chapter Ten

That was the most terrible journey I have ever made. For a whole day we sailed peacefully in a light breeze, making across the great sea, to where I hoped to find Britain, and some deserted headland on which to land and camp while we made plans. Gefwulf had said the coast was defended; but we had to go somewhere. Then as evening fell the breeze blew harder. All night it grew stronger, till by the dawn of the next day it was a raging gale, and we could no longer struggle to hold course in so small a vessel. We reefed up the sail to the smallest we could, and turning the ship's prow we let her run before the wind, helpless to stop her going where the weather would take her.

The waves washed into the boat and we were all wet and cold. The food was soaked in salt water, the drinking water fouled, and only a little less salty than the sea. We could not lift our heads without being struck down by the wind, and two of our number were washed overboard, as we fought to keep the ship bailed. The splendid suit of ring-mail, of which I was so proud on land, was cold and comfortless in the swirling waters; we were hungry and exhausted, having no shelter in our boat, and nowhere to sleep. The blood of Finn washed off my sword, but not out of my heart. I had no heart to fight the waves, no desire to live through the gale, and we would have drowned if my companions had as little taste for life as I. My torn heart rejoiced in the violence of the wild waves, and the screaming winds, glad to be driven so fast away from Finnsburg.

At last the wind dropped and we saw land. It was on the left hand, rugged and rocky, and behind the coast we could see great hills, capped with snow. We put in close, but we could not find a place to land.

'We must be far to the north, and we are lost,' I thought. 'We had better turn south where we may find a coast less harsh than this one.' So we turned about, and headed southwards. The wind had torn our sail to shreds, and it fluttered uselessly in the breeze, so we had to row. On the first night of our southwards journey we lost sight of the coast, and although some of the men wanted to turn westwards in the hope of finding it again, I wanted to keep facing south, for I thought we were more likely to find the fertile part of Britain that way. We had no sooner set our course for the south than a wind came up behind us, which would have sent us flying on our way if we had had a sail, but it blew great waves up from the sea, which only hindered our tired rowing.

We had lost count of days and nights and we were very weary. Men dropped asleep at their oars, and just lay in the bottom of the boat. Useless to try to wake them. And then on top of all the rest the wind dropped, and a mist came down. The water was glassy, and the swell heaved and fell gently without breaking the shiny surface, and all around us was a wall of white. We could not see the sun by day, or the stars by night. In a few hours the steersman did not know in what direction we were facing. There seemed no point in forcing our tired limbs to row in an unknown direction, or round in a circle perhaps. We shipped oars, and sat and drifted.

In the eerie silence round us the only noise was the slapping of the waves against the boat. I do not know how long we lay wrapped in our wet cloaks, drowsy and aching, and each in his own thoughts. Mine were of Gefwulf; of his voyage. He had been through this in winter when it must have been worse, and he had come home to that cold welcome when at last he reached land. No wonder it had made him hate us! And what landfall could we hope for? In the land of the Franks perhaps, we could land without fighting our way up the beaches. Perhaps we could take service with a Frankish lord. It seemed impossible to believe that any land in the world was real; there was only this round patch of dark sea, wrapped in white veils, and we were the only living things on the entire earth. No; there were also some birds, some sea birds, uttering their harsh cries as though to lament the emptiness. . . . I could hear their mewing now.

Then I jumped up and cried, 'Listen! I can hear the cry of gulls!' Everyone woke and listened. For gulls flock to the shores. And now we strained our ears we could hear the waves breaking on the beaches. 'What coast is this?' my companions asked. I could not tell them. We were lost so completely that none of us could even guess. But we forced ourselves to lift the heavy oars again, and steer the boat laboriously in to the shore, making towards the sound of the breaking waves.

As we did so the first wind we had felt on our faces for days came gently out of the south, swirling the white mist on its invisible current. The waves were breaking rhythmically on a wide sandy beach, and we simply rowed the boat till it grounded, and we could drop over the side and scramble out. The wind was dispersing the mist, and a golden haze of sunlight was shimmering through it. I could see that the beach sloped, and there seemed to be a green hill beyond, rising steeply above the shore. I looked back at our boat, and I could hardly

believe that we had come alive from it. It was shattered and broken, looking like a wreck, and so small that it seemed incredible that until a moment or two ago it had been the whole world. The mist was dissolving in the sun, and now I could see that the hill ahead of us was rounded, and away to the right was another just like it.

Then a single pure ray of sunlight fell upon my face, blinding my eyes, so long accustomed to dimness. I blinked, and looked down to avoid the painful glare of the bright sun. I was standing on a patch of ground brightly lit by the golden ray. The fine long grass of the salty dunes grew there, and growing in it were thick clumps of pink flowers.

Their beauty rolled back the years, and I knew where I was. I fought the knowing of it. 'No!' I cried to myself, 'No! there were three, there were three . . .' But when I looked up the mist had rolled back still further, and I could see that the mound at whose foot we were standing was indeed one of three; the one nearest the sea, the one Finn and I had climbed on long ago, when our hearts were glad. All things were well then; Finn lived and we were friends.

'No!' I cried aloud. 'We cannot land here! We must put out to sea again quickly!'

But my men stared at me in disbelief. Our ship was shattered, they were so tired that I doubt if we could have pushed her off, and in any case farther down the beach we could already hear voices hailing us, and running feet coming up. We had been seen by the sentries.

And so it was that I came to Dorestead for the second time.

How kind they were! They found us staggering about on their beaches in the last stages of exhaustion, and they called up others to help carry us to shelter. They brought us into the sentries' hut, and blew up the fires, and gave us bowls of warm milk, and dried our clothes before the hearth. All except mine that is; I dared not part with my cloak for fear that someone would recognize the mail shirt underneath, though I did not think I had seen any of these faces before. I sat still huddled in my damp mantle, and kept my head bowed. I think they thought I was crazed from the sea, for they did not argue with me, but spoke gently and patiently to me.

Someone sent to the city, and when we had sat and drowsed for some hours we heard the sound of horses outside. They had brought a cart drawn by four horses to take us into Dorestead. We were helped up to our seats in it, and gravely thanked for accepting their hospitality. To all this graciousness I made mean and brusque answer, for courtesy choked in my gorge towards these people. I have heard it said that a man hates those he has injured worse than his enemies; of me that was true indeed for a while.

The cart rolled down the path by the great river, which was shining in the sun through a light haze. It was wide, but not as wide as I had remembered it. The great walls of the city loomed over us, and we were through the gates. Here were the richly carved houses, the great streets full of bustle which I had not seen for so long, and yet had seen so often in the mind's eye only, that they were both strange and well known to me. I was certainly going up them to my death, but it was not death I feared to face, but reproach. I thought I saw among the staring people faces I remembered, but I was never sure, and it was very long ago. And then as nobody seemed to recognize me in the cart for all to see, I even wondered wildly if I might get away with lying about who I was. Murderer that I was, why should I shrink from lying?

We were given a small room to sit in and warm ourselves until the evening meal was ready, and then we were led to our places in the hall. We sat down in Goldgleamer, facing the high-seat, where we had sat long ago, and Folcwald came in and took his place above us. He was old and frail, and bent a little, but he still had a firm step and a steady eye.

'Greetings, strangers,' he said to us, 'you are welcome to our hall. Eat and drink, and listen to the song of the minstrel, and when you are rested you shall tell us who you are, and why you have come.'

Good food was set before us, and the feast began. The hum of voices rose round me. It was not as I remembered it loud with gaiety – the voices were hushed under a weight of grief. I kept myself wrapped close in my tattered mantle, and looked downwards, keeping my face from the gaze of men. My companions had given themselves up for lost, and were eating their last meal with what relish they could muster. I could see out of the corner of my eye the rich but sombre colours of the Frisians' splendid clothes, I could hear the chink of their cups and dishes. The lovely voice of a singer caressed my ears, and woke aching memories in my heart. No – I would not lie; I would tell the truth that Finn might be avenged.

A lovely young woman came and filled our cups with wine. She had the red hair of Finn's kin, and the pleasant ways which go with high rank. And when we had drunk she came over to us with a box of gifts, and gave us each some good thing from Folcwald's store. Low though I might bend my head, the gift she gave me showed they knew me for the leader, for it was the most costly – a silver bowl with a pattern of vine leaves round the rim. When she had given these things she raised her clear voice, and bade the thanes of Dorestead join with their lord in giving gifts of welcome to the strangers.

There was a sound of benches pushed back, and bustle round me. I kept my gaze fixed downwards, and saw only the feet of the thanes who came by, each laying a gift before me. Their gifts were chosen with care for men in our position; new clothes, new sandals, unbroken bottles, a keg of salt, a coil of sealskin rope, a good sail, a pair of oars, were laid before us.

My heart groaned at it. 'They know indeed that we are men of rank, or they would not give noble gifts,' I thought. At last the passing men stopped, and I heard above my head Folcwald's voice, thin and tremulous with age, but a voice of power still.

'Strangers, we hope that you are warm and rested in our hall, that you have eaten and drunk your fill, and that your hearts are gladdened by our gifts. And now if you are contented, stand and tell us who you are, and how you came here.'

There was a hush around me. My limbs were heavy, my heart was cold and it seemed to me to take all my strength to move my wasted body, so great was my reluctance to rise and speak. But the hush grew deeper, and at last the length of it forced me to my feet.

I got up, and I let my mantle fall from my shoulders, so that my ring-shirt was plain to see. And I stood and looked at Folcwald. I saw his eyes open wide at me, and I knew that he knew me even before I spoke, though none of his thanes did.

'The wind and the waves brought us to you, great King,' I said aloud, 'against our will. Dearly would we love to be elsewhere!'

'What is your name, wanderer?' asked Folcwald in a voice of icy fierceness.

'Why do you ask?' I said. 'What use is it either to tell or not to tell what is already known? I am – Hengest!'

And there I stood for all to see, for any to strike down, each inch of my flesh in the prickling expectation of the blows of dagger or sword; and after the first sounds which greeted my answer – the indrawn breath, the jumping up, the chink of swords touched by all around me, there came no sound and still came none; the assembly of the Frisians had been frozen into unnatural stillness like the waves of Finnsburg.

I stood at first fearing the death blow; and then as I stood unharmed I began to fear another thing, a worse one, I began to fear they would not harm me, and that I would have to live with the guilt of Finn's death upon me. At last the silence was broken by a running step coming up behind me. Folcwald's eyes turned from my face towards this sound and it stopped. A sigh came from the hall-thanes. I did not look. I knew without looking that a sword had been drawn against me, and that Folcwald's glance had stopped my death. And now at last Folcwald spoke.

'Whatever may be the ways of the Jutes, O Hengest,' he said, 'among the Frisians there is respect between guest and host. I did not seek to have you as my guest; it is for another reason I might have sought you. But since you come unwilling and unwanted on the unthinking storm, and are yet my guest, you have nothing to fear from me. Sit and drink, and my people shall wait upon you.'

Then slowly, and with even more reluctance than that with which I had risen, I sat down in my place. And from everywhere in the hall the Frisians got up and went out. They left their wine-cups half full and went; only the pages, the minstrel and the servants remained, and with them remained the king. Only duty could make them stay

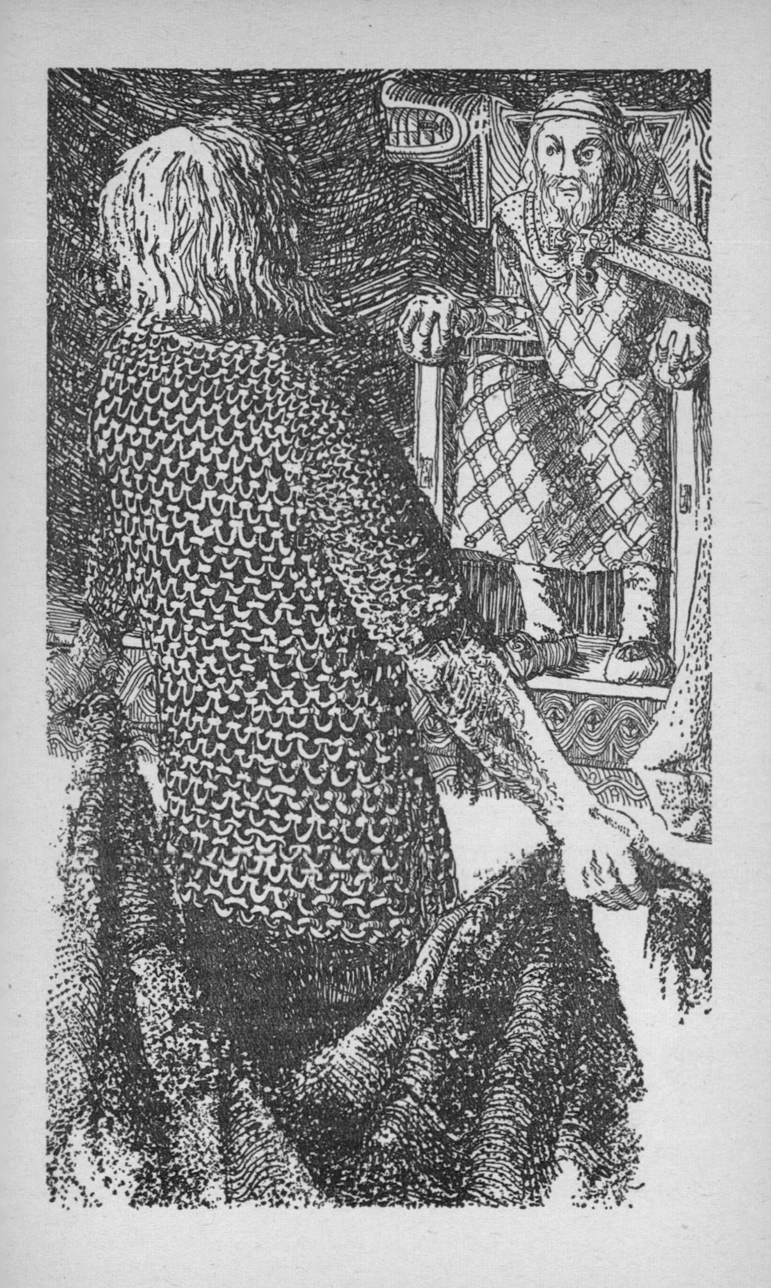

where I was. And Folcwald, finding I had no other company, talked to me.

'The wine is good, for it comes from the harvest of the south three years ago, when there was a pleasant summer. Do you not feel the sun upon your tongue? Drink more.' His words had a tone of harshness beneath their pleasant meaning and they echoed in the emptied hall. I tried to swallow more wine, and could not. I felt my gorge rising, and choked. My head swam.

'You are tired with your terrible sea-faring,' said Folcwald as though in kindness. 'Let my pages show you to your bed.'

The next day Folcwald's council met to talk about me. I discovered from the men who were set to guard me that all the Jutes in the kingdom had been rounded up and brought to Dorestead, and were held in a hall at the other end of the town, while Folcwald decided what to do with them. There were many of them; all those whom Hnaef had driven out, or who had come to seek wealth in a more promising land. These men must hate me, I thought, almost as much as the Frisians, for I had served the lord who had oppressed them, and now had poisoned their welcome here.

In the evening I was brought before the council to hear what they had concluded.

'We will not harm you, Hengest,' said Folcwald. 'We will not kill a guest. But it is hateful to us to have you, or any of your wicked oath-breaking countrymen upon Frisian soil. Therefore you will take all the Jutes who have lived here, and you will go in ships we will find for you, and you will not come back. Indeed if you set foot again upon our lands we will take the vengeance owing to my son and grandson.'

'Great King,' I said, 'I cannot lead men who hate me.

I expect your vengeance. I too grieve for Finn. He should not go unavenged.'

One of the councillors jumped up and cursed me. 'Vile man! How dare you talk of grief for the man whom you foully killed! Do you not wear even now the splendid gift he gave you? Does not your armour show you for a two-hearted traitor?'

'Silence!' said Folcwald. 'It may be as he says. Many are the ways a man can feel. Well, Hengest, if you speak the truth, I will avenge my son in letting you live. Carry your dark heart, and your ring-shirt where you will, as long as you come here never again. I will even tell you where you can go to glut your taste for bloodshed; I know a man who can use warriors. In Britain there is a king called Vortigern. He has many enemies to fight, and he asks me for help because he rules what was once a Roman province, and I am an old friend of Rome. It is but a short journey across to his island, and he will welcome any help he can get. Take your countrymen, and go to him.'

They took me to the hall where the Jutes were held, and left me with them. They were bitter against me, and they had already chosen their leader – Horsa, whom Hnaef had vanquished with my help long ago. But I had the blood of the god in my veins, and my father's name for wisdom, and I had seen more battles than he, and come alive from the teeth of great storms at sea. And they needed a leader who could deal with such things for the future threatened many perils and offered little safety. Our plight was desperate enough; it was even worse that we should be divided among ourselves. So I swore blood-brotherhood with Horsa. We cut our wrists, and let the blood fall into one cup, and both tasted it. Never have two men sworn themselves into kinship liking each killed their king in battle, to have murdered his people, or broken his treaty. Beside what I have done to Finn, it weighs with me not at all. And it has given my followers a home; for them at least I have done well; it is right that they should remember me.

There are Saxons and Angles here now, fighting for land. No matter; there is enough for all, and we who were here first have won the fairest part. Let any nation come; we can share with them. Any but the Danes. And if ever the Danes come let my people fight them with a loathing like mine!

Epilogue

That was all a long time ago; time has blurred my recollection of some of it, but not dulled the edge of pain. Bring me a drink. No, not wine, that makes my fever higher. Take my silver drinking bowl, and bring me water from the stream outside the door. I am dying now, and you must make a song out of all this, and sing it among my people, so that they will remember how their kingdom was founded. You know the rest, or can find it by asking any of my thanes.... Give me the drink then, and I will tell you.

Vortigern trusted me, because he saw that I wore Roman armour, and he took me for a friend. But he changed his mind when he saw how well we could fight. We beat his enemies, and then he scanted our reward. So we fought him instead. We won this land from him, and made it ours, or mine rather, for Horsa was killed when we fought at Aylesford. This is my people. In all that we can we make ourselves like the Frisians, because they are the noblest people I have known. And I will not be called a Jute; I hate the name for Finn's sake, and so we call ourselves Men of Kent, from the name of the land we have won.

The Britons call me hard names, saying I broke my oath to Vortigern, and killed a man whom I had taken as my lord, and have a heart of stone which shrinks not from the shedding of blood. That is all true. But for their wrongs I do not care. It is a small matter to me to have other less! But in time we learned to live and fight side by side.

Folcwald gave us weapons, and supplies, and found us ships, and was glad with all his heart to see us go. But on me he laid his curse, wishing by all his gods that I should never feel safe as guest or as host; that I should never again give or receive trust; that I should never forget what I had done; that whatever I did my two-faced heart should never find wholeness and peace.

And the gods heard him.

also by Jill Paton Walsh

The Dolphin Crossing

' "Look, son" said Crossman. "This is no kids' game. You are right about what's going on; but you haven't any idea what it is like. You would be sailing into the middle of a battlefield. They are taking men off from right under the nose of enemy guns; sitting ducks those boats will be, and no defending them possible. Let me tell you, it isn't funny being under fire. And in a boat it's worse; fire and water, either will kill you. Have you ever thought of dying, son? Really dying? Or getting your face smashed in? Have you considered losing your legs, or losing your eyes? Have you ever seen a man who's been badly wounded? I have, I saw enough in the last war to last me as long as I've got to live. You think about it, and go back home to bed." '

This is the story of two boys, and the friendship which flowered between them during the early days of the last world war – Pat and John, both knew the risks they were running, yet took a boat to help save the stranded British army from Dunkirk. It is not a true story, but it could have been true, for there really were schoolboys who helped ferry the British army in retreat. It is also truthful in another sense: when real people take real risks they get killed.

For readers of ten and over, boys especially.

If you have enjoyed this book and would like to know about others which we publish, why not join the Puffin Club?

You will be sent the Club magazine Puffin Post *four times a year and a smart badge and membership book. You will also be able to enter all the competitions. Write for details to:*